Friendship Chronicles

★ ★ ★ Starring ★ ★ ★

Pinkie Pie, Rainbow Dash & Twilight Sparkle

Written by G. M. Berrow

Little, Brown and Company
New York ★ Boston

Little, Brown and Company
Hachette Book Group
1290 Avenue of the Americas, New York, NY 10104
Visit us at lb-kids.com

Little, Brown and Company is a division of Hachette Book Group, Inc.
The Little, Brown name and logo are trademarks of Hachette Book Group, Inc.

The publisher is not responsible for websites (or their content)
that are not owned by the publisher.

First Edition: April 2016
Twilight Sparkle and The Crystal Heart Spell originally published in paperback
in April 2013 by Little, Brown and Company
Pinkie Pie and the Rockin' Ponypalooza Party! originally published in paperback
in July 2013 by Little, Brown and Company
Rainbow Dash and The Daring Do Double Dare originally published in paperback
in January 2014 by Little, Brown and Company

Library of Congress Control Number: 2016931688

ISBN 978-0-316-27259-9

10 9 8 7 6 5 4 3 2 1

RRD-C

Printed in the United States of America

CONTENTS

* * *

Twilight Sparkle

★ ★ and ★ ★

The Crystal Heart Spell

Chapter 1

A Crown Achievement

✴ ✴ ✴

All of Equestria had been celebrating since the joyous wedding of Shining Armor and Princess Mi Amore Cadenza. Cadance, as she was called, was one of the most loving mares in all of ponydom. The citizens of Equestria, including the newly recovered Crystal Empire, were living in a time of happiness and prosperity. Apples grew in the orchards, creatures big and small played in the lush green fields, and ponies of all three tribes lived in harmony. And now, another promising young royal had been inducted into the highest ranks of pony society. It seemed like the cherry on top of a delicious ice-cream sundae.

Ponies of all kinds from the far reaches of Princess Celestia's kingdom were curious about the new princess who had just been crowned. She wasn't just anypony. This was a young Unicorn pony with a violet-hued hide, a beautiful purple-and-pink-striped mane, and incredible raw abilities. Her name was Twilight Sparkle, and she was indeed very special. Stories of her amazing magical gifts had even been passed along all the way from San Franciscolt to Manehattan. These tales had started to become legendary—especially the one about the time she took on the formidable ursa minor on her own, or better yet, the time she defeated the evil Queen Chrysalis in order to save the royal court of Canter-lot. Everypony was excited to see what wonders would accompany such a unique princess's reign.

Twilight was excited, too. Not only did she bear an esteemed new title, but she had earned something unique as well. Twilight had received her very own set of wings. *Real* Pegasus wings! She was officially a part of a special breed of pony called an Alicorn. This meant that Twilight was now able to harness the magical powers of the Unicorns, the flight abilities of the Pegasi, and the strength of a good, true heart of an Earth

Pony. She was becoming more like her mentor, the talented and kind Princess Celestia, every day.

Although it was very exciting for Twilight to become an Alicorn, she didn't take her new gifts for granted. It was an honor to become part of something so rare and exclusive. She didn't care about all the shiny jewels and castle quarters she'd been given as part of the job. Twilight was happy to remain in Ponyville for now. She loved to spend time studying in her library with Spike, the baby dragon who was her number-one assistant, and having barrels of fun with her best friends. Luxurious castle furnishings could wait.

Ever since Princess Celestia had sent Twilight away from Canterlot to study and learn the magic of friendship, she had really felt that Ponyville was her true home. Twilight was uncertain how she would feel if she had to leave it. And ruling her own kingdom? That was another story.

It was true that Twilight Sparkle loved to help other ponies, to teach them the interesting facts she'd read about in the pages of her beloved books. She also enjoyed her position as designated leader of the Ponyville Winter Wrap-Up. But being in charge of the well-being of a kingdom of ponies didn't seem easy. She could tell that much from having studied with Celestia for all this time. Twilight was nervous. She still had so much to learn about being a leader. But, then again, there was *always* more to learn. Twilight never seemed to be able to acquire enough knowledge on any subject. The world was so vast and fascinating!

＊　＊　＊

One afternoon in Ponyville, just after the Pegasi had moved some clouds into the sky for a short rainfall, Twilight went home to scour every book in her library yet again. She was hoping for some guidance on exactly how a pony could become a great princess and leader. There was bound to be some information that could help a pony out. She thought she was on to something when she first laid a hoof on the pages of *The Princess Bridle*. It was one of her favorite stories about royal ponies, but not quite right.

"What about this one, Twi?" Spike exclaimed, pulling a dusty book with a teal cover from one of the low shelves. He couldn't reach the higher ones without a ladder. Twilight perused the book, titled *Purple Reign* by somepony named Crystal Ball. But that was no good, either. It just had a ton of song lyrics in it.

"Spike!" Twilight exclaimed. "What am I going to do?" She threw her hoof up into the air, exasperated. "I need somepony's help. I just know there's more to being a leader than what I already know." Twilight began to pace around and around the room in her usual manner. She did this so often that the floorboards had worn down, forming a large circle. Spike liked to call it the Twilight Zone.

Spike furrowed his scaly brow and clapped his claws together. "That's it!" He sprang up and knocked several titles from the shelf. A moment later, he appeared in the pile of fallen books clutching one with a familiar blue-and-yellow cover. Twilight recognized it immediately as *Daring Do and the Trek to the Terrifying Tower*. She had already read all the books in the series about the fearless pony adventurer at least three times. Twilight cocked her head to the side. "I don't get it, Spike. What's Daring Do got to 'do' with it?"

"Well, you know how Daring has to rescue a pony who's been locked in a tower surrounded by a moat filled with sharp-toothed piranhas?"

"Yeah...so?"

"And you know how she has to dive into the water in order to get to the tower even though fish are secretly her biggest fear?"

"Spike! Spit it out, already!" Twilight exclaimed. "Do you have an idea on how to help me or not?" She was beginning to look a bit stressed. Her mane had gone frizzy and one of her eyes was twitching ever so slightly. Twilight took her responsibilities very seriously—sometimes too seriously.

"Well, basically Daring Do wants to overcome her fears once and for all. So she asks some older ex-adventurer ponies, like Professor A. B. Ravenhoof, for tips on how to do it!" Spike spread his short arms wide in triumph.

Aha! It was so obvious to Twilight now. She needed guidance. *Real* guidance from somepony who had been around the stable block a few times. "Why didn't *I* think of that?" Twilight's face lit up, thinking of all the ponies she could interview. "Good work, Spike! It's perfect." Spike blushed. He loved nothing more than to be a good assistant to his best friend. But he could hardly say "You're welcome!" before Twilight Sparkle was out the door to find out about the great leaders of Equestria—straight from the horses' mouths.

CHAPTER 2

A Foal House

★ ★ ★

"Who in Ponyville might be able to help me?" Twilight said aloud as she trotted through the town square. Then she caught sight of Mayor Mare walking on the opposite side of the courtyard, heading into the town hall with a group of important-looking ponies. The mayor would be a good choice.

She ran their whole town! She would definitely know a thing or two about leadership. It was a good place to start.

But by the time she reached the steps of the town hall, the mayor was already behind closed doors. "Sorry, Princess Twilight," Senior Mint, the tall green guard pony said. "Ms. Mayor Mare is in an important meeting about next year's Summer Sun Celebration and won't be out for some time."

Twilight slumped in defeat. "Oh well. That's all right! But you don't have to call me, um, Princess. Just Twilight will do," she advised. Senior Mint nodded, embarrassed.

"Will you tell her I stopped by?" Twilight asked. Maybe they could talk about being a leader later.

"Yes, of course, Princess Twilight." He

cupped a hoof over his mouth. "Oops, I mean *Just Twilight*." He was clearly a bit nervous around her.

"Thanks!" She flashed her shiny white smile, turned on her hoof, and headed back to square one—wandering around the town square trying to come up with her next move. Suddenly, she smelled the scent of something sweet and scrumptious. Her tummy rumbled in response.

"Fresh cupcakes! Extra icing!" shouted Carrot Cake, the town baker. He pulled a pink-and-yellow cart filled with sugary delicacies of every flavor and color. Maybe it was time for a snack!

"Hello, Mr. Cake!" Twilight said, trotting up to the cart, which had begun to draw a sizable crowd of hungry ponies hoping to snag one of the fragrant delights. Twilight hadn't seen such a commotion since the last cider sale at Sweet Apple Acres.

Mr. Cake nodded in response. "Hiya there, Twilight Sparkle!"

"Is this your new treat cart?" she asked. "What a wonderful idea!"

"Mrs. Cake and I are always trying to come up with new ways to share our desserts with the ponies of Ponyville." Pumpkin Cake and Pound Cake, twin foals, giggled and trotted alongside their father. Pound Cake, who was a Pegasus, beat his little wings until he was hovering near a tray of pink and purple pastries. When his father wasn't watching, he sneakily snatched one and ate it in a single greedy bite. His sister, Pumpkin Cake, jumped as high as she could to grab one, but she couldn't quite reach. She finally used her Unicorn magic to steal a blue cupcake and deliver it gently to her mouth. She licked her lips with a satisfied smile. Then she burped.

"Plus, the babies love to get out of the shop," Mr. Cake continued, oblivious to his little foals' devious actions. He was too busy dishing out baked goods to the crowd of hungry townsponies. "Fresh air sure does them good!"

Twilight watched as Pumpkin and Pound chased each other. They ran in circles and through the legs of a nearby gray Pegasus pony. The pony wobbled helplessly before toppling over into a nearby rosebush. When she popped her head out, her lemon-yellow mane was adorned with prickly thorns. "Mr. Cake! Do you have any muffins today?" she called as she tried to climb out. Her hoof

⭑ **19** *⭑*

got caught on a branch, and she tumbled onto the soft grass.

"Fresh out of muffins, unfortunately," Carrot replied, looking concerned.

"Well, *I'll* take one cupcake please." Twilight licked her lips in anticipation. Mr. Cake reached inside the glass display case, but all that was left were crumbs. "Oh dear, we seem to be out of *everything*!" He frowned. His business venture was more successful than he'd expected.

"Why don't you trot back to SugarCube Corner with us?" Carrot offered. "Mrs. Cake is sure to have whipped up some more by now."

Twilight hesitated. She was supposed to be on a fact-finding mission, not lounging around Ponyville eating sweets. Her stomach rumbled again and Pumpkin Cake giggled.

"I guess that's my answer," Twilight said ruefully. "Just for a few minutes, though. Then I have to get back to my quest."

The twins cheered and hopped on Twilight's back for a ride to the bakery. "Giddy-up!" they chorused.

✳   ✳   ✳

"Mrs. Cake, this rainbow chip…*mmmf*… delight is…*mmmf*…delicious," Twilight said with a full mouth. A dollop of pink icing made its way down her chin. Rarity would have been appalled at her bad mane-ers. "Excuse me," she said as she cleaned her face. "I don't mean to eat and run like this, but I really must be on my way."

"Of course, Princess," Mrs. Cake said, bowing quickly. She stood up and continued to pipe a tube of icing onto a strawberry layer cake, creating a beautiful border of plump roses in the process.

Twilight blushed with embarrassment. "You really don't have to call me that," Twilight replied. This *princess* business was tricky. Maybe she should put up a banner in the town square telling everypony to treat her as they normally would. "I'm just the same old Twilight, really."

She caught sight of her reflection in the shiny cake display case. Other than the new wings, she still looked the same. She wasn't even wearing her tiara. "In fact, I don't really know how to be a princess at all. That's what I'm doing today. I'm trying to ask some older ponies what it means to be a leader, but I don't want to ask Princess Celestia—that would be embarrassing—and when I tried

to go see Mayor Mare, she was busy and..."
Everything seemed to spill out at once.

Mrs. Cake furrowed her brow in motherly concern. "My goodness, that sounds like quite the sticky situation. Why don't you visit your big brother and Princess Cadance?"

Twilight brightened at the suggestion. What a great idea! Her BBBFF (Big Brother Best Friend Forever) Shining Armor and new Pegasister-in-law had much more royal experience than she did. Older siblings were practically made for giving guidance. "You're a genius! They are bound to have some royal advice!"

Carrot Cake popped his head in from the storeroom. "We're not out of royal icing! We have a whole carriage full back here, my dear!"

"No, Carrot," Mrs. Cake shouted back.

"Royal *advice*. For Twilight!" She shook her head and then sighed. "Stallions. They never listen."

Twilight chuckled as she made her way out the door. "In that case, maybe I'd better talk to Cadance and *not* Shining Armor." She was feeling much more confident now that she had a real plan. "Thanks for the terrific tips and treats, Mrs. Cake! Bye, Pumpkin! Bye, Pound!" And then the young monarch was off to the Crystal Empire to find out exactly what made a royal pony tick. Or at least talk.

CHAPTER 3

Empire State of Mind

★ ★ ★

Twilight Sparkle didn't think it was possible, but the Crystal Empire looked even more beautiful than the last time she'd been there. The winding, cobble-gem streets and tall spires sparkled and glistened in the sunshine. Every facet of shining glass turned a different hue when the light danced on it. It had been a long journey, but it was well worth it to be back. As she entered through the front gates, Twilight felt a sense of overwhelming pride in her brother's new realm.

Everything appeared to be fully restored back to its former glory, partly thanks to her, of course, though she would never brag about it. The Crystal Empire had been through many dark days after the evil King Sombra tried to keep the source of the Empire's power—the Crystal Heart—hidden away. The Crystal Heart, charged by the power of the ponies' love, was the only object that was able to offer the Empire protection. Once it was stolen, the kingdom was overtaken by darkness.

Luckily, Princess Celestia had put Twilight to the test when she recruited her and her best friends to help. They came to the rescue, putting on the long-forgotten Crystal Faire while Twilight searched for the Empire's beloved Crystal Heart. When Twilight finally succeeded in recovering the precious, magical gemstone, not only did she pass her test, but balance was also restored to the stunning city.

As Twilight walked past a group of Crystal ponies, she smiled and waved. "Good afternoon, everypony!"

"Hey, Princess Twilight Sparkle!" they shouted in response. "Welcome back!"

A sparkling teal-colored pony with a light blue mane jumped up and down in excitement. The pony was named Glitter

Dance and reminded Twilight of her eternally energetic friend, Pinkie Pie. "We're going to the Crystal Lake today!" she exclaimed. "Come play with us!"

Twilight politely declined but was pleased by the invitation. The ponies were having tons of fun with one another, which was always a good sign. Every corner of the kingdom appeared to be filled with light and love. It was certainly the perfect place for Shining Armor and Princess Cadance to live and rule. Of course, having Cadance as their princess had likely contributed to the warm, fuzzy feelings of the Crystal pony population.

"Twily!" a handsome white stallion with a blue mane yelled from across the courtyard. Shining Armor hadn't seen his sister since her coronation. He galloped over and embraced her in a classic big-brother hug.

"How's my second-favorite princess?" He knocked her cheek lovingly with his hoof.

"Hey, now!" Twilight laughed. "I was around first!"

"Only kidding!" he said as Princess Cadance trotted over to join them. "You're *both* my favorite princesses."

"Cadance!" Twilight called out. "*Sunshine...sunshine...*" she started, looking to the elegant princess for acknowledgment.

"*Ladybugs awake!*" Cadance yelled in joyous response.

The two of them sang in unison as they hopped around and shook their tails at each other. "*Clap your hooves and do a little shake!*" It had been their secret tailshake since Twilight was just a little filly and Cadance was her foalsitter. It was still amusing after all these years, even though a couple of nearby ponies watched the scene in slight confusion. It was unusual to see their composed princess acting so silly.

"So what brings you to the Crystal Empire, little sis?" Shining Armor asked. "Isn't royal life great?" He beamed with pride and smiled wide. His little sister had come so far in her studies that she'd achieved princess status. It was very impressive, and he loved to tell other ponies all about her accomplishments. But ever since she was crowned, it was no secret to anypony. Twilight was famous all across Equestria now.

"Well…that's sort of why I'm here." Twilight dropped her eyes to the ground and scuffed a hoof around. "I'm not good at being a leader of other ponies. I don't know how to act! I don't feel anything like a princess, and it's just weird to have everypony call me that. I don't feel very graceful.... Not like you, Cadance."

"Oh, Twilight!" said Shining Armor. "It isn't an easy transition. But you are doing great!"

Twilight knew he was trying to help, but she couldn't resist rolling her eyes a little bit. "Of course you would say that. You're my brother—you have to think so!"

"Chill out, Twily. Being royalty is a cinch! Right, Cadance?" He was clearly missing the point.

Cadance's face became serious. "No, Shining Armor. It's not as simple as that. I completely understand what she's going through." She turned to her fellow princess. "Maybe I can help you, Twilight."

She started by leading Twilight Sparkle down the street and through the city. Twilight was happy to follow.

CHAPTER 4

A Tail to Tell

★ ★ ★

It was a busy day in the Crystal Empire. The streets were bustling with Crystal ponies rushing home from the markets and shops, their packs filled with fresh apples and other luxuries.

"Good afternoon, Moondust!" Cadance

greeted an iridescent white pony with a sleek silver mane. She was selling baskets of Crystal berries (an Empire specialty) at a little stand near the fountain. "How are your foals doing?"

The pony beamed as she bowed to the two princesses. "They are wonderful! Would you like some fresh Crystal berries?" Moondust asked, and gave them each a small bunch. The sweet tartness exploded in Twilight's mouth as she devoured them. Twilight made a mental note to bring some back for the Cakes. The berries would definitely taste delicious in a pie.

"Thank you very much!" Twilight said as they walked away. How did Cadance do that—remember the names of a whole kingdom's residents? Twilight sometimes found it difficult to remember the names of just the entire Apple family. So far in the Empire, she'd met Topaz Twist, Citrine Star, Rosie Quartz, and now Moondust! Cadance's memory was impressive. Twilight wondered if she studied every night.

"I always try to remember everypony in the kingdom, because each one is special," Cadance explained as they walked. "We all play our part in making the kingdom a happy and fun place to live." Twilight sighed. Cadance definitely had a point, but all these new responsibilities were starting to add up. Maybe she could make flash cards with each pony's picture on it.

"You're such a great princess, Cadance," Twilight said. They approached a young Crystal pony couple, who smiled and bowed as the princesses passed them. "I wish I could be like you. I feel so lost."

"You know," Cadance offered, "I didn't always feel so confident."

"You didn't?" Twilight asked, trying to think of a time when Cadance had seemed as lost as she felt now.

"When I was found as a baby Pegasus, in a forest far, far away..." Cadance began the familiar tale. Twilight listened intently as Cadance recounted her path to becoming the great pony leader she was today.

Cadance told her how some Earth Ponies from a nearby village took her in as their own little filly. And as she grew up, the natural love and compassion she had for others filled everypony with warmth and the urge to protect her. Cadance was definitely special.

But all was not well for long.

An evil pony enchantress named Prismia lived alone nearby. She rarely came out of her cottage because she felt nothing but jealousy for the other ponies in the village—the way they loved and took care of one another. And yet, she had nopony who cared for her. Prismia always wore a powerful necklace, which she cared for more than anything else in the world, and it served to amplify the evil and jealousy within her own heart. When Prismia's bad feelings and the power of the necklace finally overtook her, she cast a spell on the villagers that leeched all the love from their homes. She hoped to capture some of that love for herself. Everypony was distraught and sad.

Cadance decided that she couldn't let that happen, so she went to see Prismia. Luckily, the enchantress's powerful necklace also amplified the power of Cadance's love, and she soon defeated Prismia with her incredible gift of compassion. Once Prismia changed her horrible ways, Cadance was surrounded by magical energy and transported to a strange place—a place that nopony except Princess Celestia had ever been! So when Celestia discovered special little Cadance in that mysterious location, her fate was sealed. The princess brought her back to Canterlot to raise her as her very own royal niece—the special and loving young Princess Cadance.

Princess Cadance's special talent had always been her amazing ability to spread love wherever she went—settling conflicts and bringing ponies of all kinds together. In her final exam at Celestia's school of magic, Cadance was even able to make two known rival pony families of Canterlot become best friends for life.

"So I spent a long time in Canterlot just resolving conflicts whenever I was needed and helping other ponies find love. I never really experienced it for myself." Cadance blushed a little and giggled. "Even though I *did* have a crush on your brother."

Twilight made a disgusted face. "Yuck."

"Everyone was telling me what a great princess I would be someday, but I just didn't feel like I knew what to do!" Cadance said. Twilight nodded in enthusiastic agreement. Now they were talking. "So I went to Princess Celestia for advice."

"And . . . ?" Twilight asked, all ears.

"She asked me if I *felt* like a true leader." Cadance stopped walking and turned to her young companion. "I told her that no, sadly, I didn't."

"And...?" Twilight repeated again. She could hardly take the suspense!

Cadance continued, "She told me about an ancient spell that had the power to make anypony who was destined to lead become the pony they were meant to be."

Twilight smiled. She *knew* that there was an answer to all of this—and of course it was a spell!

True leadership was only an enchantment away.

✶ ✶ ✶

The two ponies soon found themselves standing in front of a giant crystal statue of Cadance. The sun shone through it, creating hundreds of tiny rainbows in the water flowing through the fountain. "Wow, they must… really love you a lot here, Cadance." Twilight cocked her head to the side. She could never imagine having a statue of herself. It was a bit much.

Cadance shook her head and shrugged. "Oh, I guess so!" she said, chuckling.

The famous, powerful Crystal Heart stood next to the statue, shining brilliantly with the magic of the Crystal ponies. Thankfully, it was safely displayed right where Twilight had last left it, rather than hidden away with some evil king. Rescuing the heart once had been difficult enough. She didn't want to have to do it again.

"So where can I find this leader spell, then? Can you teach it to me? Is it in one of the old spell books?" Twilight asked eagerly.

As soon as she learned the words from Cadance, she'd be on her way back to Ponyville. Then everything would be solved.

"Oh, no, Twilight." Cadance shook her head. "This spell isn't something that can just be learned. The Crystal Heart Spell can only be revealed when a future leader of Equestria understands what her biggest challenge in leadership will be. Only then will she know how to rule, in her heart."

Twilight furrowed her brow in confusion. What in Equestria was Cadance talking about? *Revealed*? Twilight was somehow supposed to get some random spell to appear out of thin air? This was going to be trickier than she'd expected.

"How in the hoof am I supposed to do that?!"

"I can help you with one clue, just as

Celestia did with me." Cadance's voice was gentle and reassuring. "Just think about the elements that make up a great kingdom, Twilight."

"The Elements of Harmony?" Twilight asked. It was the first thing that popped into her mind, so it probably was too obvious.

"Not exactly…" Cadance said. "What are the best things we have in Equestria?"

Twilight cocked her head to the side, completely baffled. Cadance thought it might be time for a different approach. So she began to recount her search for the spell in greater depth. Cadance warned Twilight, though, that the spell worked differently for everypony. It couldn't be repeated.

"Once I received the clue myself, I decided to start by asking my friends what they thought," Cadance remembered. "They had all sorts of crazy ideas about what they liked in a kingdom."

"Like what?" Twilight was soaking everything in like a sponge. This would all be useful in helping her find the Crystal Heart Spell.

"Well, my friend Buttercream said she thought every kingdom should have a chocolate fountain in the center. And another pony I knew, Sky Chariot, suggested a curfew time for all ponies to be home by." Cadance scrunched up her face in distaste. "I didn't really agree with any of them, but I used their ideas anyway."

Twilight nodded along as she listened to the story.

"But nothing happened!" Cadance said

dramatically. "The spell was nowhere to be found, and I was more lost than ever."

Twilight's eyes grew wide. "So how did you find it?"

"One day, I was sitting by the lake just outside Canterlot, reflecting on the situation," Cadance recalled. "I thought about how all I had ever done was listen to the suggestions or commands of other ponies."

"Like the way they would always ask you to help them fall in love?" Twilight asked.

"Yes, exactly! I never made any decisions for myself." Cadance stared out into the water of the crystal fountain. "As soon as I realized this, the spell appeared, shimmering in gold letters on the surface of the lake."

"Wow..." Twilight cooed, imagining the

pretty scene. Maybe she should go visit the Crystal Lake after all.

"As soon as I read the spell aloud, I instantly knew that my destiny was to lead other ponies with my strengths of True Love and Tolerance. But the only way to do it was by listening to my *own* heart as well."

A gift Horse

★ ★ ★

Cadance led Twilight through a massive wooden door and into a lush castle bedroom. It was decked out in rich, royal velvets of deep purple and gold. Hundreds of precious gems of every color adorned the bed frame and hung from the chandelier. The early-evening light shining through tall, gilded windowpanes was dazzling. It raked across the gray and silver stones of the walls and onto the lavish furnishings. With all the glitz, the castle quarters would have suited Rarity perfectly. The only thing about it that screamed "Twilight" was the fully stocked bookcase in the corner.

Twilight blinked her eyes in disbelief. "This room is all mine?"

"Well, not *all* yours!" Spike popped out from behind the purple drapes and did a little vaudeville dance. "Surprise!" Cadance laughed at the little dragon's antics.

"Spike!" Twilight exclaimed, and instantly felt guilty for leaving him behind earlier. "Sorry I left Ponyville in such a rush. You know how I get when I'm on a mission."

"Do I ever!" said Spike. "It's just lucky

you came back here when you did. I almost ate that entire bed frame while I was waiting for you." Spike's eyes grew large with longing as he looked around the room. Jewels and crystals were his favorite meal. It had taken a lot of self-control to keep from nibbling the furniture.

"Good thing you didn't." Twilight's eyes landed on a small, wrapped golden box with a bow on top. It was sitting in the center of the bed. "Spike, you didn't have to bring me a present. It's not even my birthday!"

"But I didn't...." Spike scratched his head. "I don't even know where that came from!"

"It's from me," Cadance said, nudging it toward Twilight with her muzzle. "Just a little gift from one princess to another." Cadance winked.

Twilight tore open the packaging. Inside was a beautiful necklace made of purple jewels. At the center was a large, prismatic gem in the shape of a heart. It had a special quality to it that Twilight had seen only one other place... around Cadance's neck!

"Cadance, is this your favorite necklace? From when we were growing up?" As a filly, Twilight had admired the necklace. It had always seemed to be extra special in some way that she couldn't quite put her hoof on.

Cadance smiled warmly. "Of course it is! I think it's time that a new princess wore it proudly."

"Oh, Cadance!" Twilight put the necklace on and spun around. Spike's eyes were glued to the adornment. Twilight admired herself in the mirror. "I'll take such good care of it! Thank you."

"Of course, my dear new sister," Cadance said as she made her way to the door. "I just want you to know one thing."

Twilight was still spinning around in front of the mirror, dreamy-eyed. "Yes?" she said, though it didn't seem like she was paying much attention.

"The rare gem in the middle has been enchanted with a powerful charm," Cadance explained. "As long as the pony wearing it is filled with the magic of love and positivity, the necklace will wrap her in warmth and protection."

"It sounds amazing!" Twilight said, looking down at the rare gem in awe. "Wait, is this the same necklace from the story? That Prismia wore?"

"It very well may be," said Cadance with a wink before she turned serious again. "But you must also remember that if the pony wearing it does *not* display those traits, it will only serve to magnify the negative thoughts and doubts within her!" cautioned Cadance. "Be careful, Twilight. Remember: If you stay true to your heart, the spell will soon reveal itself." And with that, Cadance was gone.

"Got it!" Twilight replied lazily, exhaustion from the long journey finally beginning to overtake her. She climbed into the cushy bed and nuzzled down into the covers. In the morning, she would begin to look for the elements of a perfect kingdom. "True to your heart..." she whispered before falling into a sweet, dreamless slumber. It was the sound sleep of a princess with a purpose.

* ✶ *

She'd only been there a day, but Twilight Sparkle's Crystal Suite was already a mess. All the books from the shelf in the room were pulled out, littering the floor and bed. Some were open to pages filled with spells and history lessons; others lay closed in stacks. Spike sat on the window seat, gazing out at the panoramic view of the Crystal Empire and then looking closer with a telescope. He was trying to guess how many crystals were out there and also how yummy each one would taste.

"Where did Cadance say she started looking for the spell?" Twilight asked Spike, who hopped down and started restacking the books onto the shelf. It was almost like being back home in the cottage.

"I don't know!" Spike replied. "I was up here waiting for you, remember? I didn't hear her story."

Twilight wandered over to the box that held her gorgeous new necklace. It was sitting on a beautiful dresser with a mirror. As soon as she slipped on the necklace and looked in the mirror, she knew exactly what to do. "She asked her friends for their opinions—that's what Cadance did!" Twilight exclaimed. "Spike, take down a letter! No—make that *five* letters! I'm going to hold a secret spell summit with my best friends."

A meeting of the greatest minds in Ponyville was just what she needed to crack this case wide open.

CHAPTER 6

On a Scroll

* * *

Spike had been extra busy all day delivering the invitations for Twilight's emergency secret meeting. He'd visited Fluttershy's cottage first. She politely accepted and asked Spike if he wanted to come inside and play with her new fruit bat, Toby. "He's ever so shy, and I think he could use a new friend like you, Spike," she said in her tiny, gentle voice.

"Sorry, Fluttershy! I have all these scrolls to deliver for Twilight. Maybe Toby and I can 'hang out' later!" Spike chuckled at his own joke, but Fluttershy looked confused. "Get it? 'Hang out'? Because bats hang upside down?"

"Oh yes, of course. See you at the meeting!"

Next, he found Applejack working in the orchard at Sweet Apple Acres. She bucked her hind legs against a tree and a batch of juicy apples came tumbling down into a basket. "A meeting for Twilight?" Applejack looked relieved. "Phew! Nopony has seen her around for a few days! I was about to send out the Apple family search party."

"Did somepony say *party*?!" An excited

Pinkie Pie popped out from behind a tree. "Because my Party Watch just went off!" She held up her hoof to show Spike and Applejack a bright neon accessory. It looked like a watch, but instead of numbers it just had pictures of colorful balloons, streamers, and confetti with the word *party* spelled out twelve times. Little blinking lights rimmed the edge, and a honking noise was being emitted from a tiny speaker at the top.

"But where are all the numbers?" Applejack asked, confused.

"Who needs numbers?" Pinkie said, and shrugged.

"To see what time it is, silly!" Applejack threw her hooves in the air to illustrate her point.

"But it does tell the time! It's party time… all the time!" Pinkie shouted with glee. "Now who said the magic word, huh? Huh?!" She came up to Spike and looked him straight in the eye. "Was it you?"

"It's not a party, really...but here you go, Pinkie." Spike handed her a scroll. She quickly unfurled it and read the message. "A secret meeting party?! Oh goody, goody gumdrops! I have to go get ready!" And then Pinkie Pie bounced off toward her house.

"Thanks, Spike," Applejack said, shaking her head. "I guess you can count me and Pinkie in."

Rarity, on the other hand, was less thrilled about the invitation. She peered down at the scroll through her purple cat's-eye work glasses. "I'm in the middle of making a huge order of hornaments! Can this wait until later?" Rarity was always try-ing to finish some new garment or accessory for her Carousel Boutique. She was a very hard worker.

"Twilight said it was an emergency." Spike looked down at his feet. He didn't like to upset Rarity, because he really, really liked her. But she always responded to a few well-worded compliments. "Say, Rarity…have you done something special to your mane? It looks super-duper shiny today!"

"Well, actually, I did go to the spa this morning to have my hooves done and they gave me some new conditioner…." Rarity began to ramble. Five minutes later, Spike was still standing there. "…and then I said, 'Darling, if you must do my tail as well, just do it.' I knew it would be worth it!"

"Well, it looks great! Gotta run!" Spike quickly said before heading off down the road. He had spent quite a bit of time listening to chatter about the latest beauty treatments in Ponyville, and now he was running late. Luckily, he had only one stop left. Rainbow Dash was the last pony he had to invite to Twilight's secret meeting.

"Special delivery for one Miss Rainbow Dash!" Spike shouted halfheartedly at the clouds. He was ready to call it a day by the time he reached Ponyville Park. It was directly under Cloudsdale, so there was a good chance of finding the Pegasus there. "Rainbow Daaaash!" he called out impatiently. "I have a very important invitation to a very secret meeting at Twilight Sparkle's cottage!"

"Hold your ponies, Spike," Rainbow Dash said, swooping down from a cloud. "I'm comin'!"

Rainbow zoomed by a cloud that looked empty, but hidden inside was nosy Gilda the Griffon—and she had heard every word!

Suddenly, the "secret meeting" was not so secret.

✶ ✶ ✶

"So what in tarnation is this all about, Twi?" Applejack asked as she bit into one of the apple fritters she'd brought for the meeting. All five of Twilight's best friends had shown up, even though surely they had other important things to do. Twilight knew she was lucky that they'd come to help her, no questions asked. It filled Twilight with a sense of pride and warmth that made her new necklace shine doubly bright.

Twilight cleared her throat and looked

at each of the ponies in the circle. "Thank you all for coming—" she began, and was immediately interrupted by Rarity.

"Is that divine necklace around your neck made of Cosmic Spectrum?" She stared at Twilight's new accessory with desire. "I have only seen pictures of it in books! My goodness, it's gorgeous! It almost looks like a mini version of the Crystal Heart." Rarity trotted over to get a closer look.

"Thanks! It was a present from Princess Cadance."

"You know what they say about Cosmic Spectrum..." Rarity added, turning to the other ponies. "When you wear it, you must remember—"

"Oh, totally. Yeah, I know all about it," Twilight said in order to keep the meeting moving. Twilight didn't want to listen to

Rarity talk about gemstones right now. The clock was ticking! Rarity shrugged, a little hurt. She trotted back to her spot and plopped down.

"*Anyway,* thank you all for coming on such short notice." Twilight looked around at each of her friends with genuine gratitude. "I've asked you here because I desperately need your help—"

"Ooooh! I know!" Pinkie Pie interrupted with a squeal. "You're planning an undercover jewel-heist mission and you want us all to join 'Sparkle's Six'?"

Twilight shook her head. "Not exactly, Pinkie."

Pinkie Pie was wearing a tan trench coat and a fedora hat in an attempt to disguise herself for the meeting. She had also brought along a drink she called "Secret Punch" as a refreshment, but she wouldn't reveal what the ingredients were, because it was a "super big secret." As a result, nopony wanted to drink it. "Or…you volunteered to plan this year's Hearth's Warming Eve pageant and you need us to help?!"

"Pinkie, it's still summertime," Rainbow Dash said, rolling her eyes. "I don't think that's it."

"Whatever it is, can we just get started?" Rarity whined. "I have lots of work to finish back at the boutique! Those hornaments are due in Mythica, Neigh York, by tomorrow morning and they aren't going to finish rhinestoning themselves. Do you have the time, Pinkie?" Rarity motioned toward Pinkie's Party Watch.

"Sure!" Pinkie said, and looked at her wrist. "It's 'party.'"

"Pardon me?" Rarity didn't quite comprehend. Applejack and Spike couldn't help but giggle, since they knew what was coming. "The time is party?"

"*It's party tiiiiime!*" Pinkie cheered, and did a skipping lap around the room. Everyone laughed except Rarity, who just looked annoyed.

"Okay, everyone! That's enough," Twilight said. "Down to business."

The ponies finally listened as Twilight recounted her trip to the Crystal Empire, sparing no details. She told them all about Cadance's journey to find the Crystal Heart Spell. Twilight explained that the only way she herself would find it was with the help of her friends. Just like Cadance.

"So I'll need you all to come up with some ideas for my future kingdom. If you don't, I'll never find the spell and I'll never learn to be a leader and I'll never be a great princess!" Twilight said in one breath. She had the tendency to exaggerate things.

"Calm down, Twilight," Fluttershy said, patting her on the back. "I'm sure that we can all figure this out together."

"Together?" Twilight asked hopefully. "You'll help me?"

The rest of the ponies nodded and held up their full cups of Secret Punch in a toast. "Together!"

Brainstorming the Castle

★ ★ ★

The six ponies had been brainstorming forever, but Twilight somehow felt like she was even farther away from finding the spell than before. The conversation kept going in circles. They all seemed to have very different ideas about what they would do if they were in charge.

"There should be an official Cake Day!" Pinkie said, licking her lips. "Everypony in the kingdom just eats cake all day like a giant birthday party!"

"A royal guard made up of the fastest Pegasus ponies would be totally awesome," Rainbow Dash chimed in. "We could hold a race to find out who's the best." Then she pointed to herself. "Other than me, of course."

Twilight took note, but knew this was not the sort of information she was looking for. She sighed heavily. "Applejack? Rarity? Any thoughts?"

Applejack's eyes lit up. "Oooh! How about making everypony have dinner with their families every night like the Apple family does?" she said earnestly. "Strong families build a strong community."

"Okaaay," Twilight said, thinking of her own brother and parents and how far away they lived. It was a nice thought, but it wasn't a practical suggestion. Not everypony was lucky enough to live near their family like Applejack.

"I have an idea!" Fluttershy offered.

"You do?" Twilight replied, her ears perking up. Fluttershy was soft-spoken, but she could be very creative and surprising. "Tell me!"

"I was just thinking how great it would be if there were a place where all the baby animals could play together in safety, far from the scary creatures of the Everfree Forest. Like a nature reserve, but just for baby animals! That's what I would do." She stared dreamily out the window, imagining playing with all the adorable animals.

"Ummm…okay," Twilight said, and wrote down the idea.

Twilight was starting to rethink her plan. She needed real ideas about how a kingdom works, not silly ones about baby animals and cakes. "Rarity, any ideas? You've been awfully quiet over there."

"Well, sure. If you *actually* want my opinion now…" Rarity grumbled. Ever since she'd tried to warn Twilight about the necklace and was shut down, Rarity hadn't felt like saying a peep. "I would design a fashion line, just for the kingdom. Exclusive pieces made from extravagant fabrics so that everypony would look and feel their best!"

Pinkie Pie and Fluttershy nodded in excited agreement, but Twilight wasn't impressed. "Fashions, Rarity?" Twilight shook her head in defeat. "Come on, you guys! Think outside the box!"

"Well, sorry if my idea wasn't good enough for you, *Princess*," Rarity replied, and stuck her nose in the air. "I wish you luck in coming up with a better one." Then she trotted out of Twilight's cottage in a huff.

"Whoops," Twilight said, finally realizing she had hurt Rarity's feelings. "I didn't mean to make her feel bad. Guess I got a little carried away. Sorry, everypony. I guess that's enough for tonight."

CHAPTER 8

Gilda's got game

★ ★ ★

Gilda the Griffon waited patiently outside Twilight's cottage until the last pony had left the secret summit. Pinkie Pie had hung around for ages giving her friend suggestions for different holidays to start and celebrations to throw.

"Thanks, Pinkie," Twilight said as she

walked her to the door. "I'll certainly consider making Gummy's birthday an official holiday." Gummy was Pinkie Pie's pet alligator.

"Great!!" Pinkie squealed. "He'll be so excited when I tell him the news!"

All of a sudden, a crazy noise started sounding from Pinkie's watch. "Gotta go, Twilight! I totally forgot about the housewarming party at Berry Punch's new place!" With that, Pinkie bounced off into the distance, singing a song. *"Oh, the bestest cottage is a warm one! A cottage that is filled with frieeends! So let's warm this house and fill it up with a party that never eeeends!"*

"Finally! I thought those ponies would never leave," Gilda said, swooping down from a cloud and landing softly in front of Twilight. "Productive meeting, Twilight?"

"Hey! How did you know about the meeting?" Twilight asked suspiciously. It was supposed to be a secret.

"I have my ways," Gilda said, pacing around Twilight. "And I listened to the whole thing. Didn't sound like your friends had *any* good ideas for your kingdom...."

"So what, Gilda?" Twilight sassed back. "You think you can do better?"

"I'm just trying to say that if *I* were a princess like you—I wouldn't be listening to anypony's suggestions. I would do whatever I wanted! Make my kingdom all about Gilda!" The griffon cackled and flew off into the clouds again to cause some mischief elsewhere.

Twilight brushed it off. Nopony in their right mind would take advice from Gilda, the notorious bully. Twilight still trusted her best friends the most. And why shouldn't she? They had proven themselves to be honest and loyal.

But then again, they didn't have years of magical study with Princess Celestia under their belts like Twilight did. And her friends had never even lived in Canterlot, so it was silly to expect them to know very much about being royal.

Twilight went back inside her cottage and looked into a large cerulean-colored chest. It was filled with her new gowns and jewels from the coronation. None of it seemed like hers. Twilight removed a tiara from its velvet case and placed it gently on her head. She looked in the mirror. The sparkling white diamonds and red rubies shone brilliantly. The tiara made her stand a little taller.

Maybe Gilda had a point. Maybe the

secret to leadership was listening to your own heart instead of everyone else's. Isn't that what Cadance had said?

If she was going to be a real princess, maybe she just needed to start acting like one.

✶ ✶ ✶

The aimless search for the Crystal Heart Spell was beginning to wear on Twilight, even though she was doing her best to try to act like a princess. She still didn't know where or how to look for it. It was making her crazy!

She even felt like she was hearing voices, which was never a good sign. For example, that morning in the Ponyville marketplace she'd asked Cheerilee which type of berries she should buy. Cheerilee had suggested the blackberries, but Twilight could've sworn she'd heard a voice coming from a stack of crates saying, "Who cares what *she* likes? What kind of berries do *you* want, Twilight?"

Later, when Twilight was looking after the Cutie Mark Crusaders—Apple Bloom, Scootaloo, and Sweetie Belle—she'd heard it again. They'd all been in Ponyville Park, deciding what afternoon activity to partake in. Twilight was getting frustrated because she really wanted to read the fillies a story from one of her favorite books, but all they wanted to do was jump rope. She was sitting by, watching them, when she heard the voice again. "Look at them!" it whispered. "You know what's best for them and they didn't even listen to you. You're the *princess*, for Celestia's sake!"

She'd looked around but hadn't seen any-pony who could have said it.

It was so odd. Ever since Gilda the Griffon planted the idea in her head that she shouldn't listen to her friends, Twilight had started to feel that everyone else's opinions were wrong. But was Gilda right?

Twilight decided to trot through the forest in hopes of clearing her head. The serene green trees and silence were usually comforting and helped her work out any problem she was having at the time.

She was only alone for a few moments, however, before a loud crash signaled the presence of another, familiar pink pony.

"There you are!" Pinkie Pie shouted through the trees. "I have been looking aaaall over for you! I want to show you my awesome plan for the new kingdom's holiday celebrations…and also play and hang out and eat cupcakes and all that super-duperiffic great stuff!"

"Thanks, Pinkie. But now isn't a good time," Twilight said calmly. "I'm sort of busy taking a walk." She motioned to the leafy path ahead of her.

"Okay! Will you be busy in ten minutes?" Pinkie asked, walking alongside her and smiling wide with excitement.

"Yes," Twilight replied. She was really starting to get frustrated now. She wanted be alone.

"Okay! What about in twenty minutes?!" Pinkie asked. She thought everything was a game.

"No! I'm busy now, I'm busy in ten minutes, and I'm busy in twenty minutes. I'm busy *all* of the minutes!" Twilight snapped. Her necklace began to dim, the colors churning. "Can't you see I don't have time to talk about your silly little parties?"

"What?" Pinkie Pie slumped to the ground, hurt. "Sorry to bother you, Twilight. I was just trying to help. I guess I'll leave you alone and go where somepony wants me."

"Finally!" Twilight sneered. "That's the best idea you've had yet!" As she trotted off into the distance, Pinkie began to wonder what was really going on with Twilight Sparkle.

This time, she didn't think it was something a party could solve.

CHAPTER 9

A Head in the Clouds

✦ ✦ ✦

Twilight Sparkle was planning to ask Rainbow Dash if she'd seen Gilda the Griffon anywhere. Even though the two of them were no longer the best of friends, Rainbow always saw most of the comings and goings of the residents of Ponyville. There were great views of the whole town from up in the clouds, so she might know.

Maybe talking to the griffon again would shed some light on the situation. There had to be more to what she tried to tell Twilight the other night after she crashed the secret meeting. Or maybe not. But a princess should listen to everypony, Twilight told herself. Especially because she still hadn't thought of a way to find the spell.

Rainbow Dash was sitting on a cloud high in the sky. She appeared to be arguing with a large group of Pegasi. She didn't hear Twilight trying to call her from below. *Good thing I have wings now*, Twilight thought, taking off. She enjoyed the rush of cool air as she soared into the sky. It was fun to be an Alicorn!

"I have herded more clouds today than

all you slowpokes put together!" Rainbow Dash shouted at the other Pegasi. "My skills are second to nopony!"

"If you're so good, Rainbow Crash, why don't you help out the rest of us?" a big stallion named Hoops shouted back. His cutie mark was three basketballs.

"Rainbow!" Twilight called out, but Rainbow didn't notice.

"You asked for it!" Rainbow shot back at Hoops, and took off into a showy barrel roll. She gathered a nearby cloud, combined it with two others, and then jumped onto it. A heavy flood of rain poured out the bottom of the massive cloud like a waterfall.

"Just call me Commander Hurricane!" Rainbow yelled, grinning from ear to ear.

"Rainbow Dash!!" Twilight yelled a little louder. Why wasn't Rainbow listening? A princess was trying to speak to her! Twilight frowned. "Rainbow! Listen to me!"

Rainbow Dash finally noticed her friend hovering there, looking a little strange. "Oh, hey, Twilight! Are you here to talk about my awesome plans for the new royal guard?"

"No." Twilight rolled her eyes like answering Rainbow's question was really hard work. "Have you seen Gilda?" Rainbow cocked her head to the side. Twilight was acting really weird, and the colors on her necklace were swirling around.

"Are you okay?" Rainbow asked.

"Of course I am! Now, have you seen Gilda or not?"

"I think she's down by the farm with Trixie," Rainbow said. "The two of them have been spending a lot of time together lately. If you ask me, it smells like trouble. Mixing pranks and magic is a bad idea, right, Twilight?"

But Twilight Sparkle didn't hear the last part, because she was already off, flying toward Sweet Apple Acres. She didn't even say "thank you."

CHAPTER 10

Drinking the Lily Pad Slime

✦ ✦ ✦

A good patch of leafy foliage was always ideal for spying. That was precisely the reason why Twilight Sparkle often found herself hiding behind tree trunks and peering through hedges while doing various sorts of field research.

Today, Twilight crouched low behind a

bush near the barn at Sweet Apple Acres. She had spent the last ten minutes watching as Gilda and Trixie rolled a barrel of fresh cider from the stacked-up stores and dumped it onto the grass. *Glug, glug, glug.* The cider spilled out quickly. Why anyone would waste the precious cider was beyond Twilight's understanding. Yet the two of them snickered as they began to fill the empty barrel with some gloopy green gunk that resembled the lily pad slime from Froggy Bottom Bog.

"These ponies will never know what hit 'em!" Gilda laughed triumphantly. "This might be one of my greatest pranks yet!"

Trixie joined in. "And once the unlucky ponies who get a cup of 'cider' from this barrel take a sip, I'll swoop in and perform a magnificent spell to save them from the horrible taste!" She cackled.

"Personally, I think it's funnier not to save them . . . but whatever you want, Trix!" Gilda said. "This partnership is really working out." The two of them high-fived.

"Hey!" Twilight shouted from the nearby bush. "You two!"

Gilda and Trixie scrambled to cover up the barrel, and both stepped in front of it to create a shield. They looked all around but didn't see anyone until Twilight climbed out from behind the bush. A couple of wayward twigs were still stuck in her mane.

"What are you, the undercover cider police?" Gilda sneered. "Do you take all your orders from Applejack now? Or are you finally giving some orders of your own, like a real royal pony, eh?"

Twilight puffed up. She was a little bit offended. "Well, if you *must* know, I couldn't

★ ✲ ★ **99** ★ ✲ ★

care less what you do with that cider," Twilight said, even though she knew she would definitely tell Granny Smith which barrel was filled with slime later. "But I'm here because...because...I wanted to ask you about..." Twilight couldn't seem to find the words to ask Gilda the Griffon for help.

Trixie tapped her hoof on the grass impatiently. She was still wearing her purple magician's robe and pointy hat covered in stars. "The Great and Powerful Trixie doesn't have all day, Twilight!" She was clearly still a little bitter about the time Twilight accidentally revealed her to be a fraud in front of all of Ponyville. Trixie probably didn't feel so "Great and Powerful" after that.

"What were you talking about the other night at my cottage?" Twilight asked Gilda.

The griffon crossed her arms and

shrugged casually. "I was just saying that if *I* were a princess, nopony would be allowed to tell *me* what to do." Gilda put her claw on Twilight's shoulder and dug in a little too sharply. "What is it that *you* want to do, Twilight?"

"I want to..." Twilight hesitated. It was a little strange to be asking for Gilda's opinion on the matter. But she *was* right. Why was Twilight spending all this time and energy trying to listen to her friends in Ponyville, when she herself knew exactly where to find the answers—the one place she always felt completely at ease, no matter where in Equestria she was? "I want to go to the library! The Crystal Empire Library!"

Gilda nodded in satisfaction. "I'll admit— the library thing is a little weird. But the Crystal Empire sounds awesome! Right on,

Princess Twilight! You always know what's best."

A moment later, Twilight's jeweled necklace began to cloud and darken even more. The transformation was so brief and subtle that Twilight didn't even notice.

But there was definitely a new determination in her eyes. And it was a little scary.

All that Twilight could think about now was that huge library in the Crystal Empire. It held hundreds of old books! There was no way the spell wasn't hidden in the pages of one of them. She couldn't wait to dive into her studies and hide away with her books for as long as it took.

"Thanks for your help, guys," Twilight told Gilda and Trixie. "I have to go to the Crystal Empire right now!" Twilight spread her wings and took off into the air.

"That sounds so totally awesome! I'm coming, too," Gilda said, flying alongside her. "Is everything really made of crystals? What are the ponies like there?" Gilda began to imagine all the innocent victims whom she could play her pranks on. It was going to be so funny!

"Trixie will go with you, too!" Trixie exclaimed, trotting beneath them. She pictured a whole new city of ponies who had never seen her "Great and Powerful" magic act yet. It was going to be glorious!

The two lackeys followed as Twilight soared through the air, winding through

Ponyville and unaware of everything in her path. Fluttershy, who was leading a line of baby ducklings back to their mother at the pond, noticed Twilight approaching. "Oh, hi, Twilight!" she said very quietly. She smiled and waved. "I'm so glad you're here! I came up with some new ideas for the baby-animal sanctuary that I wanted to share with you...."

But Twilight didn't even see her and swooshed right past. She was going so fast that Fluttershy's pretty pink mane blew out from the gust of wind Twilight's wings created. Rarity watched the scene unfold in pure shock. Who was this pony and what had she done with their best friend, Twilight Sparkle? Twilight always stopped to talk with her friends. Then Rarity noticed that the Cosmic Spectrum gem on Twilight's necklace had lost some of its luster. This was a bad sign.

"Oh, Fluttershy!" Rarity said, trotting up to her. She was carrying a large sketchbook in her pack. It was full of new outfit designs she had been drawing all morning for Twilight's imaginary kingdom. Even though she'd been annoyed after the meeting, she still wanted to help her friend.

"Do you think she heard me?" Fluttershy squeaked sadly. "Twilight would never ignore somepony like that on purpose, right?"

But before Rarity could mention the necklace, Gilda the Griffon called out to them. "Twilight is a princess now, you guys! She's off to the Crystal Empire and doesn't need a bunch of silly Ponyville friends like you holding her back. She told me so herself. So leave her alone!" Then she took off into the sky after Twilight.

Rarity and Fluttershy exchanged a worried look. "We'd better go find Spike," Rarity said, looking to the sky. "He'll know what to do."

CHAPTER II

Rallying the Hoofs

✦ ✦ ✦

Golden Oak Library looked like it was occupied—the lights were on inside. But Rarity and Fluttershy had knocked on the door three times and got no answer. "Is any-dragon home?" Fluttershy whispered, her voice barely audible, as usual.

Rarity scoffed. "You're never going to get

his attention like that! Watch and learn, darling." She stood up straight and cleared her throat.

"Spiiiiike! Are you theeeeere?" Rarity trilled into one of the front windows. A split second later, Spike flung open the door. "Hi, Rarity!"

Fluttershy wasn't offended that Spike hadn't greeted her. Everypony knew Spike had a major crush on Rarity. At least it had gotten him to open the door. He was holding a large tub of ice cream and looked like he'd been crying.

"Are you okay?" Fluttershy asked.

"Twilight left me behind again!" Spike wailed. "She went back to the Crystal Empire and didn't even tell me! I had to hear it secondhand from Cranky Doodle Donkey. He said he was walking by Sweet Apple

Acres on his way home and heard her talking about the trip with Gilda and Trixie."

"Unfortunately, it's true," Rarity said, entering the cottage. "We saw her leave."

"No good-bye or anything," added Fluttershy. "Just whoosh! And gone."

"I think we can all agree that Twilight has not been herself today," Rarity said. Spike and Fluttershy nodded. "And I think that necklace is to blame!"

"Huh?" Spike and Fluttershy were equally confused.

"Last night I was trying to explain that even though Cosmic Spectrum is a beautiful gem, it can be very dangerous if it is exposed to too many negative feelings. It absorbs them and makes the pony wearing it feel worse!"

"Oh no!" said Fluttershy. "Poor Twilight."

"I knew it wasn't her fault!" Spike jumped up in the air. "We have to go save Twilight. Together?"

"Together!" shouted Rarity and Flutter-shy. They all nodded in agreement. Now all they had to do was find Rainbow Dash, Applejack, and Pinkie Pie and explain to them what had happened. The sooner they rallied the troops, the sooner they could hop on the Friendship Express to the Crystal Empire for a rescue mission.

CHAPTER 12

Crystal Clear

★ ★ ★

"Look, I don't care what the two of you do—" Twilight snapped at Gilda and Trixie. "Just stay out of my way and don't make any trouble!"

Twilight was almost to the Crystal Empire Library when she ran straight into Shining

Armor. "Twily? I thought you went back to Ponyville!"

"I did, but now I'm back again!" Twilight said, shifting from hoof to hoof anxiously. She was itching to look through those books. She just knew the answer was in there somewhere.

"Great! You should come have lunch with me and Cadance in the castle," Shining Armor said.

"That's so nice, but I don't have time—maybe tomorrow. I have to go! Talk to you later!" Twilight said, cantering past him.

He watched in confusion as she ran off down the street and around the corner. Normally, she was excited to see him. It was very odd behavior, especially for Twilight....

Shining Armor took off toward the castle.

He had to find his wife, and he had to find her fast!

* * *

It was a familiar scene for Twilight, sitting in an accidental fort made up of large, glittery books. She hungrily flipped through the pages of one called *Ancient Spells of the Crystal Empire: Volume Four.* After the first three volumes, she had begun to feel discouraged, but she soldiered on. The Crystal Heart Spell just had to be in there somewhere!

"Twilight! Are you in here?" Princess Cadance called out, her voice echoing throughout the cavernous library. Shining Armor had come to her straightaway after seeing his sister act so bizarrely. Something wasn't right, and he knew Cadance could help.

"Yes, I'm in here," Twilight sighed loudly from inside her book fort. She didn't want to see Cadance right now. She felt embarrassed for not making any progress at all with the spell. Cadance peeked through a gap in the precarious towers of books.

"Oh dear, Twilight…" Cadance shook her head. "It's just as I suspected."

"What is?" Twilight whined. "Me being as big of a failure as I am? A pony with no leadership skills whatsoever?" Twilight hung her head in defeat. "Celestia should just go ahead and revoke my crown now."

"No, no, no. You're not a failure," Cadance said. She pointed her hoof at Twilight's neck. The Cosmic Spectrum wasn't shining at all anymore. "Look! You've gotten so down on yourself and those around you that the necklace is magnifying your negative feelings!"

The young princess looked down at the gem, stunned. "I didn't even notice that the necklace had changed...." Twilight suddenly thought of all her friends back in Ponyville. Rarity had tried to warn her about the gemstone, but Twilight had been so distracted trying to find the spell that she didn't even listen.

Actually, Twilight had dismissed all of their ideas. She suddenly thought of Pinkie Pie's cake day, Applejack's family dinner time, Rainbow Dash's Pegasus royal guard, Fluttershy's baby-animal sanctuary, and Rarity's kingdom fashions. The ideas didn't seem so bad now. Her friends were only trying to help her, like she'd asked them to.

And how did she thank them? By ignoring them and thinking only of herself.

"Oh, Cadance, I've been so horrible to my friends!" Twilight said, standing up. Several nearby books toppled over like a set of building blocks. "All I have been doing is thinking about what I want and not listening to anypony else's ideas!" The necklace began to glow dimly. "I have to go find my friends right now and apologize!"

Princess Cadance grinned as she watched Twilight gallop out of the library. She knew Twilight was on the right track again.

PFF to the ReSCue

★ ★ ★

"Where do you think she'll be?" Applejack said as the five ponies and their baby-dragon companion made their way through the front gates of the Crystal Empire. The last time they'd all visited was during the Crystal Faire. Everything looked just as pretty and shiny as it had before.

Rarity sighed, satisfied by her sparkly surroundings. "Why am I not a Crystal pony?" she lamented, remembering how her coat had become temporarily glittery when they'd recovered the Crystal Heart. Unfortunately, the effects had worn off.

"What's that?!" said Pinkie Pie, pointing to a large crowd of Crystal ponies gathered near the fountain. "Whatever it is, it looks like fun! I'm gonna go see!"

All of a sudden, a bright flash of white illuminated the sky. *Pop!* A loud noise rang out. It came from the direction of the crowd. "Come on, everypony!" Applejack shouted, leading the way.

Applejack shoved her way to the front. A red-and-white-striped tent was set up. Massive posters hung on the sides, praising the talents of THE GREAT AND POWERFUL TRIXIE, MAGICIAN EXTRAORDINAIRE. Gilda the Griffon stood outside the tent on an old apple crate. "Step right up! Step right up, Crystal ponies!" Gilda shouted, "Get yer tickets now! Step right up to see Equestria's most talented Unicorn—the Great and Powerful Trixie! Only three bits each!"

A yellow pony with a golden mane handed Gilda her money and entered the tent. Pinkie Pie looked around excitedly. "Oooooh! Does anypony have three bits I can borrow?!" She jumped up and down.

"Don't they know it's a scam?" Rainbow Dash said in disbelief. "I can't believe this!"

Gilda continued on, unaware that the Ponyville crew was standing in the crowd.

"Trixie is so powerful that she once defeated an ursa major—all by herself!"

A couple more Crystal ponies paid Gilda and entered the tent.

"Hey, that's not true!" said Fluttershy. "It was Twilight who did that. Well, she took care of an ursa minor, anyway."

"I can't stand by and watch this anymore," Applejack said. She trotted to the front of the crowd and hopped up onto another crate. "Crystal ponies! Do not pay to see this show! This griffon and Unicorn are con-ponies who are trying to steal your bits!"

A low murmur broke out through the crowd.

"What are you doing here?!" Gilda spread her wings and screeched. "First you don't know how to take a hint when Princess Twilight wants to get rid of you! And now you are ruining our show? You five are the worst ponies in all of Equestria!"

Trixie peeked out of the tent to see what was going on. The Crystal ponies all watched the scene with their jaws open. This was more of a show than they'd bargained for!

"Nopony wants you guys here!" Gilda yelled. But she couldn't have been more wrong.

"That's not true!" A voice pierced through the crowd and interrupted the argument. "They are my best friends, and *I* want them here!" Twilight broke through the mass of Crystal ponies and trotted over to her friends.

"What are you guys doing here?" Twilight asked. She couldn't believe they had come all this way.

"We came to rescue you, silly!" Pinkie Pie said matter-of-factly.

"I told them all about the necklace," Rarity explained. "We knew that you weren't being yourself."

"The Twilight we know would never be mean to her friends!" Fluttershy said.

"Or ditch us for those two!" Rainbow Dash added, motioning to Gilda and Trixie. The two of them were now bickering over whether to continue on with the show.

"I'm so sorry, you guys! I thought that listening to my own heart meant choosing whatever things *I* wanted in the kingdom." Twilight smiled, and the necklace began to glow. "Now I know that a princess is not defined by the things she chooses for her kingdom. All that matters is how she treats other ponies, especially her friends." She leaned over and pulled them all into a group hug. "Princess or not—we are all equal ponies!" Twilight said.

"Oh my, Twilight!" Rarity squealed. "Look at your necklace!"

Sure enough, the gem began to glow brighter than ever before. The light was low and pulsating, like a true beating heart. Nearby, the Crystal Heart grew brighter as well. It was almost as if the two jewels were linked by some invisible force. The ponies watched in awe as a gigantic, glittery rainbow suddenly burst forth from the center of the Crystal Heart. It arched directly into Twilight's necklace!

"Ooooooh..." everypony watching the scene cooed.

"Hey, look at that!" Rainbow shouted. "There are words on the Crystal Heart!"

Twilight knew it right away. The Crystal Heart Spell had finally revealed itself to her. She trotted over and admired the words, which were lit up in shimmery gold. She took a deep breath and began to read them aloud:

"Friendship is the creed.
It has been from the start!
It's the only way to lead—
with your Crystal Heart!"

Twilight's coat sparkled as the spell took its effect on her. *Of course!* she thought as she read the words. Friendship had always been the answer to her problems. Why did she think it would be any different once she became a princess? Twilight looked around at the crowd of Crystal ponies cheering her on, her best friends standing next to her, and her brother and Cadance looking proud.

Twilight finally felt like a real princess.

"Happy Cake Day, everypony!" Pinkie Pie shouted with glee, skipping through the center of Ponyville. Since returning from the Crystal Empire, Twilight had started using all of her friends' suggestions as practice for being a real leader someday. It was working out perfectly. Everywhere Princess Twilight looked, pony families were enjoying the special Crystal berry cupcakes and pies together. "Happy Cake Day!" they said to one another happily.

The Cutie Mark Crusaders had even made a banner that read PONYVILLE CAKE DAY! and hung it across the front of the town hall. "Great idea, Princess Twilight!" Mr. Cake shouted from the treat cart. "These things are selling like hotcakes!"

"They are hotcakes, dear." Mrs. Cake laughed.

"Don't thank me!" Twilight said, walking over to where her friends sat on the grass, enjoying their own Crystal berry cakes. "Thank Pinkie Pie! She has the best ideas!"

Twilight took a small bite of her cupcake, careful not to let her tiara fall off her head. Wearing it still took some getting used to, but everypony in town really liked it when she did. "In fact, *all* my friends have the best ideas."

Rarity smiled and winked at her. "So do you, *Princess* Twilight. So do you!"

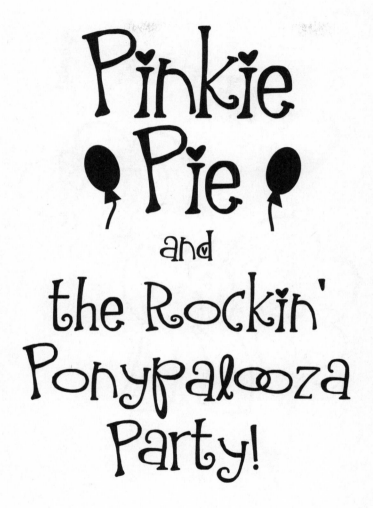

CHAPTER 1

Welcome, Spring-Sproing Springtime

★ ★ ★

It was a perfect day in Ponyville. The clouds finally cleared from the sky and gentle rays of sunshine illuminated every cottage, garden, and cobblestone path. Ponies all around town emerged from their homes, blinking the sleepy winter out of their eyes. It had been almost a week since they'd finished their annual Winter Wrap-Up. The ponies had spent an entire day working hard to clear the paths of snow and ice, welcoming back the critters, and plowing the fields to ready them for crops of fresh fruits and veggies. Now every morning was like opening a present! The ponies loved being greeted by flowers and butterflies, rather than snowflakes and chilly breezes.

This morning, one pony in particular was feeling an extra spring in her step.

"Waaaaaaaaaake up, citizens of Ponyville!" Pinkie Pie hollered, throwing open her bedroom window on the tippity-top floor of Sugarcube Corner. She was oblivious to the early hour. Even though nopony was awake enough yet to listen, she called out, "It's going to be an awesome day!"

The candy-striped curtains rustled as a sweet, fresh breeze floated inside. Pinkie closed her eyes, inhaled deeply, and smiled from ear to ear. "Don't you just love spring, Gummy?" Pinkie bounced around her pet alligator with glee, her curly fuchsia mane puffing up. "It's all sunshine and good smells and playing outside!"

Gummy blinked his large eyes in response, but his face remained expressionless. "Here! Smell this! It'll make you feel all flowery-powery!" Pinkie plucked a purple posy from her newly installed window box and bounded back over to Gummy. The tiny gator opened his mouth, clamped down on the posy, and swallowed.

"Ooooh, what a fun way to welcome spring, Gummy! Maybe I'll try it, too."

Pinkie plucked another bloom and popped it into her mouth. Her face twisted into a sour look. It did *not* taste like a sugary delight. "Yuck! Actually, maybe I'll just stick to cupcakes for now."

Pinkie trotted across the brightly colored room. Everything in sight was patterned with hearts or balloons. "So, what's on the PPP for today, Gummy?" She looked over her Pinkie Party Planner on the wall. It had been a gift from Twilight Sparkle and was where she kept track of all the exciting parties happening around Ponyville. The majority of them were events she'd planned herself, but it still pleased her to see how much fun everypony was having. Ever since she accidentally multiplied herself in the Mirror Pool in an attempt not to miss out on anything, she thought it was best to keep track of fun another way.

She scanned the list. "Let's see...Ice-Cream Sundae Sunday party at Sweetcream Scoops's house? No, that's tomorrow. Silly me! Today is Saturday." She looked at Saturday—but what Pinkie saw there horrified her. There weren't *any* parties on today's schedule. Not one! Pinkie's jaw dropped, and she sunk to the floor like a wilted flower. How could this be? A whole day with no fun activities to attend? What was she going to do with her time? The sweet sound of birds chirping outside taunted her. Even the birds sounded like they had a party planned for today!

Pinkie stood up straight with a determined look in her eye. "There's no way we can waste such a prettiful sunshiny day doing *nothing*, Gummy!" She leaped over to a mountainous stack of colored boxes in the corner—her party supplies—and started to riffle through them rapidly. Neon streamers flew through the air. Glitter confetti sprinkled down. Pointed party hats, noisemakers, and birthday candles rolled across the floor. It looked like Pinkie's party cannon had exploded! She was making a big mess, but she didn't care. Pinkie Pie needed inspiration.

"Aha! This could be superiffic...." Pinkie squealed, pulling out a shiny magenta cape edged in blue and yellow ribbons. She threw it over her shoulders and popped on a matching mask. "A superpony party, perhaps?"

Gummy blinked, unconvinced. Pinkie's shoulders sagged. He was right. The cape wasn't quite doing it. Pinkie tossed it onto the pile of rejected items and sighed. "I know! I know!" she said, brightening up again. "How about a Capture the Flag tournament? Those are fantilly-astically fun!"

Pinkie grunted as she struggled to push a massive gold box labeled PARTY FLAGS! (1 OF 3) to the center of the room. She placed a small ladder on the side and dived head-first into the box, causing several flags to spill out and land on the already cluttered floor.

Pinkie wasn't just looking for any old flag. She wanted a special flag that would be absolutely perfect for the game, and she knew just the one. It was a keepsake from the time she'd been in charge of the flügelhorn booth at the Crystal Faire. It had a sparkly pink flügelhorn on it. Sparkles were very popular in Equestria lately—ever since the Crystal Empire had returned.

But it was no use! Pinkie found checkered racing flags, some Summer Sun Celebration flags, and even flags with tiny flags painted on them. But no pink flügelhorn. Pinkie was pretty down on her luck today. "Oh well. Never mind that!" she exclaimed. "I'm sure there's something else around here...."

Meanwhile, Gummy climbed on top of one of Pinkie's homemade Super Spring Sneakers—a set of shoes with giant silver springs attached to the bottoms for maximum bounce-ability. He slowly sprang up and down on one of them, and the shoe made a small squeaky noise. It was hard to tell if he was having fun, since he couldn't smile, but he kept doing it, so that was a good indication.

"Gummy, you're brilliant!" Pinkie shouted. She did a celebratory twirl that rustled up some stray confetti like a party tornado. "Why didn't you say something sooner?!" Pinkie smiled extra wide and strapped on her sneakers. "We're going to have a Spring-Sproing-Spring Party to welcome the new season! We have so much to do!" And with that, Pinkie bounced out the door and into action. It was time to get this party started!

CHAPTER 2

Pinkie's Party Ponies

✶ ✶ ✶

Whenever Pinkie Pie went somewhere, it usually took her much less time than other ponies. She had a unique way of traveling. She preferred to hop, skip, or bounce rather than trot or walk. Today, with her spring-loaded sneaks strapped to her hooves, she was bouncing high into the sky. "Hellooo!"

she chirped as she poked her head through a cloud, surprising a green Pegasus with a yellow mane who had been asleep.

Boing! B-b-ba-doing! Boing! B-b-ba-doing!

Within a few minutes, Pinkie accidentally found herself on the outskirts of Ponyville. "Whoopsy-doodles! I overshot my bounce range again!" She giggled before heading back to the spot where she had meant to land—right in the center of Ponyville. It was the absolute best spot to start telling everypony about the Spring-Sproing-Spring Party. Then she would quickly go cottage to cottage, leaving plenty of time to set up for the party and have the best time ever the rest of the day.

Pinkie cleared her throat and looked out into the now-bustling marketplace. She began to sing and do a bubbly dance routine. "It's spring! It's spring! What a wonderful thing! It's time to laugh; it's time to sing! But most of all…it's time to spriiiiiiiing!" Pinkie Pie spread her hooves out wide and smiled at the crowd.

But nopony had stopped to listen. That didn't stop Pinkie. "You're all invited to my Spring-Sproing-Spring Party! This afternoon! By the lake! Be there if you like having a little fun, a lot of fun, or even just medium fun!"

Sea Swirl and Rose trotted past, giggling and shaking their heads. They were used to seeing Pinkie act silly, and seemed to be too busy to stop and hear what the party was all about. Pinkie shrugged and started her song again. "It's spring! It's spring! What a won—"

All of a sudden, a little voice interrupted her.

"A party? Can we come, Pinkie?" said Apple Bloom in her cowgirl accent, jumping up and down like a baby lamb. She was just a little filly—light yellow-green with a bold pink mane. She hadn't received her cutie mark yet. As usual, her two best friends, Scootaloo and Sweetie Belle—also "blank flanks," were standing by her side.

"Of course!" Pinkie shouted, and sprang into the air. "Everypony's invited! Especially you three!"

"Yay!" the three ponies chorused, and erupted into a tizzy of excitement. Parties in Ponyville were a frequent occurrence, but they weren't usually called out as guests of honor.

"What sort of awesome stuff will there be at the party?" asked Scootaloo. "Will there be bouncing?"

"Will there be springing?" added Sweetie Belle.

"What about sproinging?" squealed Apple Bloom.

"All of the above!" shouted Pinkie, her smile growing wider by the second. "And also big huge trampolines, a bouncy barn, and bundles of bungees! All of the springiest things there are." Pinkie looked at them proudly.

"Well, count the Cutie Mark Crusaders in," said Apple Bloom. She turned to her two friends. "Maybe one of us will get our cutie mark while we're there!"

"Yeah!" Scootaloo chimed in. "My hidden talent could be...jumping?"

"Let's find out!" Pinkie pulled three sets of mini spring-loaded shoes just like hers seemingly out of nowhere. It was almost like magic, but it wasn't—it was just Pinkie. She was prepared for a good time, and nopony could blame her for that!

"Wow, these are for us?" Apple Bloom took a pair and put them on her hooves. She hesitantly gave a little bounce and nearly lost her footing. It wasn't as easy as Pinkie made it look!

Pinkie's face became serious. "I need you to help me out. Everypony in town looks so busy, but I don't want them to miss this beautiful new spring day! Can you go around Ponyville and spread the word about the party while I get everything ready?"

"We'll do it!" the Cutie Mark Crusaders said in unison. They loved a new challenge, especially if a party awaited them at the other end.

"Awesome!" Pinkie replied with a jump.

"I've always wanted some Party-Planning Ponies!"

The three fillies puffed up with pride.

"Okay." Pinkie pointed to Sweetie Belle. "You start by finding your sister. Go!" Sweetie Belle nodded and bounced toward Rarity's home and shop, the Carousel Boutique. Rarity was probably there right now, working on some new outfits.

"Scootaloo, you head toward Rainbow Dash's cloud and tell her about the party so she can tell everypony in Cloudsdale!" Scootaloo nodded and started off. She couldn't fly yet, but the bouncy shoes gave her a little more height with each step. Scootaloo flitted her tiny wings hopefully and disappeared into the distance.

"And you, Apple Bloom," Pinkie said, looking down at her little filly friend, "are in charge of rounding up the entire Apple family! Yippee!"

"Aw, man," said Apple Bloom, scuffing the dirt with her hoof. "Can't I go somewhere different than my house? Somewhere excitin'?"

Pinkie cocked her head to one side, pondering this. Of course Apple Bloom didn't want to go to Sweet Apple Acres—she spent every day and night there! "You make an excellent point, Apple Bloom," Pinkie agreed. "Going to *new* places is way more fun! Why don't you take the path to Fluttershy's and stop at Twilight's library on the way?"

"I'm on it!" Apple Bloom was off before Pinkie could say "Meet me by the lake!"

Pinkie smiled in satisfaction. She was glad that her little Party Ponies understood how important the party was going to be.

CHAPTER 3

The Road
Less Sparkled

★ ★ ★

Before heading to Sweet Apple Acres to invite Applejack, Pinkie decided to take a mini detour. She would first stop by Cheer-ilee's house, Sweetie Drops's cottage, and Cranky Doodle Donkey's place. (Just in case he wanted to play, for *once*. He usually didn't, but Pinkie always asked anyway. It was the right thing to do.)

As Pinkie Pie bounced up the cobblestoned path to Cheerilee's house, humming an upbeat tune, she noticed something shiny on the ground. Pinkie bent down from her tall shoes to examine the mysterious glimmer. "I spy with my little Pinkie Eye, something SHINY!" Upon closer inspection, she saw that it was none other than a rich red ruby! Sunshine reflected off its facets and made it appear extra gorgeous next to the dull gray rocks of the path.

"Wowza!" exclaimed Pinkie. "Sparkly-warkly prettiness!" Getting excited over a ruby made her feel like Rarity, who had a special talent for finding precious stones with her magic. Pinkie had many talents, but that wasn't one of them. Yet there was the little stone—just sitting on the path. But what was a ruby doing there? How peculiar....

Maybe somepony had dropped it! Pinkie looked around. There wasn't a soul in sight. "Come with me, little ruby!" Pinkie said to the stone. "I'll help you find your owner again. I bet somepony is missing you real bad!"

Pinkie tried to pick it up, but the ruby wouldn't budge. Pinkie pulled and twisted every which way, but it remained stuck to the ground. Suddenly, she let go of the gem and toppled hooves over head into the nearby hedge. Her springy shoes had bounced her backward!

Pinkie popped out of the bush and looked again. The ruby really was stuck to the path.... But why? Just then, Pinkie noticed lots of other sparkles all around her. The path seemed to be dotted with colorful gem-stones wedged between the normal gray, black, and white rocks. They looked like rainbow sprinkles on a giant cupcake. It was such a pretty sight!

"Ooooh...ahhhh..." cooed Pinkie, her smile widening in genuine delight. "What a fun new way to spruce up a front garden." Pinkie started to hop from stone to stone, looking down at the spectrum of precious gems in awe. "Hey there, Emerald! How's it going, Sapphire?"

Just then, a mauve-colored pony with a light pink mane and a cutie mark of three smiling daisies opened the door. "Pinkie Pie!" she called out. "I thought I heard somepony outside."

"Hiya there, Cheerilee! I was just talking

to your gems!" Pinkie bounced over. "Your front path is like a party under your hooves!"

"Thanks, Pinkie! I just installed it. New garden gems from the Crystal Empire. I didn't want to be one of those ponies who follow all the Canterlot trends, but this one is just so lovely." Cheerilee smiled shyly. She was usually a no-frills sort of pony, but apparently even she couldn't resist some glitz and glamour once in a while. Pinkie wondered if Rarity had caught onto the trend yet.

"Abso-tootley-lutely!" Pinkie agreed, bouncing up and down. Cheerilee gave Pinkie's springy shoes a strange look. It wasn't out of the ordinary to see Pinkie wearing something different, but this was especially odd.

"So, what brings you to my house this morning?"

Pinkie smiled. "Well, since you asked…do you like having a little fun, a lot of fun, or even medium fun?!"

Cheerilee considered the question. "Well, I guess if you are twisting my hoof, I'd have to choose 'a lot of fun.'"

"Guhhh-reat!" Pinkie answered. "Because you're invited to my first-ever, totally awesome Spring-Sproing-Spring Party! It's to welcome spring, and it's guaranteed to be any level of fun you want!"

Cheerilee laughed. "I'll be there." Pinkie's constant enthusiasm was pretty contagious, even if a bit tiring. "What would Ponyville do without all your parties, Pinkie?"

Pinkie shuddered at the thought. Imagining a Ponyville with no parties was horrible. "It would probably be really, really, really boring!" she said, snapping out of her daydream. "See ya later, Cheerilee! Bring friends! Bring bunnies! Bring bouncy things!"

As the excited pony took off, it was hard to tell which thing shone more—the pretty path or Pinkie Pie herself.

CHAPTER 4

The Spring-Sproing-Spring Party!

★ ★ ★

"What in Equestria will Pinkie dream up next time?" Twilight Sparkle said to Fluttershy. "Look at this place!" The two pony friends stood on the sidelines of the

Spring-Sproing-Spring Party, taking in the splendor and warm spring sunshine.

As Pinkie had promised, the whole area by the lake was decorated in a springy theme. Corkscrew streamers and ribbons hung from the trees. Three massive pink trampolines were set up, along with a bouncy barn, jump ropes, a big bin of bungees, and a bunny bed. It was, indeed, the springiest place anypony had ever seen.

"I can't believe Pinkie Pie put all this together in just one day! She's so talented," Fluttershy said in her soft voice. "And Angel Bunny sure is having fun with his friends." She pointed to the area where about twenty-five bunnies were hopping up and down on a mattress, giggling. Nearby, Rainbow Dash was taking her turn on one of the trampolines.

"And look at Rainbow over there," added Applejack, trotting up and joining them. "She sure knows how to put on an excitin' show!" Rainbow did a triple backflip, and all the ponies waiting in line cheered.

"Totally cool, Rainbow!" squeaked Scootaloo. Rainbow Dash was her idol, and Scootaloo thought anything she did was awesome.

"Do it again!" shouted Lemon Hearts, a yellow unicorn with a sky-blue mane. Rainbow didn't miss a beat. She called out, "You think that was cool? I can do another trick that's at least forty percent cooler!"

A moment later, she launched herself into another triple flip routine that would have shamed any circus pony. She jumped high into the sky, burst through a fluffy cloud, and somersaulted back down to the trampoline—all without the use of her wings. The crowd cheered once more.

"Wheeee!" Pinkie Pie bounced up to her friends, still wearing her shoes with the giant springs on them. "Hey, girls! Isn't this party hoppin'?" Pinkie began to laugh. "Get it? *Hoppin'!*"

"You could say that, all right," replied Applejack. "I think I'm gonna go for a jump on that bouncy barn. Looks almost like the one we have at home! Except it's inflatable."

"Of course it does! I designed it based on the one at Sweet Apple Acres. You wanna know why? Huh? Huh? Huh?!" Pinkie asked, nodding her head. "Because he's the friendliest barn I know. You sure raised him well, Applejack!"

"I wasn't aware you knew a lot of barns

personally, Pinkie," Twilight joked. It amused her that Pinkie was now making friends with buildings, along with everypony in town. What was next? Hanging out with vegetables? A picnic with trees?

"Oh, I *do*," said Pinkie. She began talking really fast. "You'd be surprised! Let's see...there's the rock farm barn, the barn at Nana Pinkie's, the barn at Granny Pie's—that one's a *little* grumpy—and a gazillion trillion more!" Her mane was puffed up to full height, which meant that Pinkie was very excited. Either that, or she'd just been jumping a lot. Or both. "So, have you guys tried any of the super-fun activities yet?!"

Rarity, who had joined them in the middle of Pinkie's barn speech, sighed loudly. "Oh, you know I normally would, darling, except I just can't stand the thought of having to fix my mane afterward. Jumping and perfect hair do *not* go together!" She flicked her shiny purple coif to illustrate her point and trotted off to go check out her reflection in the lake.

"Okeydokey-lokey!" Pinkie replied, unfazed. "Catch ya later, Rarity!"

Twilight shrugged, then watched as Spike dived off the bungee platform, laughing as he sprang back up like a baby dragon–sized yo-yo. "Well, Pinkie, I'd say your Spring-Sproing-Spring Party is a smashing success," she said. "It seems like everypony in town is here! Even someponies I've never seen before. Like that group over there." Twilight gestured toward the bouncy barn where an older couple stood with their two daughters.

The old stallion had a light brown coat and gray mane with long sideburns and wore an old-fashioned pilgrim hat and tie. His wife had a light gray coat and wore her dark gray mane tied up in a tight bun, along with glasses and a stern expression on her face. The two young mares with them were different shades of gray. Their manes were both bone-straight, but one of them had her bangs cut evenly across and the other had hers flipped over the side of her face. They looked at each other and then frowned at the festivities going on around them.

Twilight furrowed her brow, wondering why the family was acting so odd. "Maybe they are new to Ponyville, or they are just passing through?" Something about their look said that these weren't really urban ponies. They seemed so confused and lost.

The two young ponies looked up at the large inflatable barn like they'd never even seen one before.

"New ponies? Oh boy, oh boy! Where? Where?!" shouted Pinkie Pie, darting across the field. She loved nothing more than welcoming new residents to town and learning every single thing about them. A pony could never have too many friends! Pinkie ran back and forth, scanning the crowd until her eyes landed on the group in question. The smile on her face instantly grew to maximum Pinkie happiness.

"I don't believe this!" Pinkie screamed with joy. She bounced up to the top of the bungee platform and pulled out a glittery pink megaphone. "Fillies and gentlecolts! Your attention, puuuuh-lease!"

Everypony stopped jumping and turned

to Pinkie for her big announcement. "I'd like you all to welcome to Ponyville...my FAMILY! Look, look! It's really them!" Pinkie threw confetti onto the crowd of townsponies and a cheer rang out. "See?! That's my mom, Cloudy Quartz, and my dad, Igneous Rock! And my two sisters—Marble Pie and Limestone Pie!" The crowd craned their necks to get a look at the newcomers.

"That's Pinkie Pie's family?" Spike said to Twilight. "But they don't look anything like her!"

"Maybe they are one of those families that are similar in other ways," Twilight suggested. They did look a bit plain to have such a kooky daughter like Pinkie. But families came in all shapes, sizes, and colors.

"Yaaaaaaay! Familyyyyyy!" Pinkie jumped onto one of the trampolines, using it as a launch pad to land right in front of her sisters. Pinkie couldn't believe how her luck had turned around today. She loved parties and she loved surprises. . . . But a visit from her parents and sisters at one of her parties? That was the biggest surprise of all!

CHAPTER 5

Between a
Rock Farm and
a Hard Place

★ ★ ★

Her family all wore blank expressions as
Pinkie skipped and twirled with glee. It was
obvious that Igneous Rock had dealt with
Pinkie's exhausting energy many times before
when she was a filly. He stood patiently for a

while, waiting for her to calm down. But soon he grew tired of the act, and his face morphed into a frown. "All right, now," he said. "That's enough." But Pinkie was too excited to notice his disapproval.

Meanwhile, Twilight, Applejack, Fluttershy, Rainbow Dash, and Rarity stood close by. They'd heard a lot about Pinkie's days growing up on the rock farm, but they'd never actually met Pinkie's family before. Some of the other party-going ponies started to gather around, too. Apparently, they were also curious to learn more about the relations of the most popular pony in town. Chances were good that her family was probably totally fun, too.

"Hi, Mom! Hey there, Dad! How's it going, Marble? What's new, Limestone? Where's—?"

"Your older sister is keeping an eye on the farm," Igneous cut her off.

"Oh, okay. So what are you guys doing here?! I'm so totally surprised!" Pinkie skipped around her family. "My Pinkie Sense didn't warn me about this at all! Are you here to party? I planned all this! Look, there are lots of really cool—"

"Pinkamena Diane Pie," Igneous interrupted. "We are not here to party."

Pinkie stopped in her tracks. "Oh. You're not?" She cocked her head to one side.

"No," Cloudy Quartz replied. Marble and Limestone shook their heads solemnly.

"Well, why'd you show up at a party, then, you bunch of silly heads?" Pinkie giggled and nudged her mother. "A party is the absolute *worst* place to *not* party!"

A couple of ponies laughed. Pinkie did have a pretty good point there.

"Pinkamena, don't you start with me...." Cloudy warned, looking down at Pinkie through her glasses. Pinkie shrank back.

"Sorry, ma'am," Pinkie said, her mane deflating a little. "I just got really excited to see you guys. It's been super-duper long! I mean, you guys never even leave the rock farm. Oh no—is something wrong with Rockie?!"

"Who's Rockie?" Cloudy asked, growing impatient.

"Rockie's my pet rock, Mom! He's gray and a bit lumpy and about yay big?" Pinkie made a motion with her hooves to demonstrate the size of the rock in question. "I definitely introduced you to him."

"Oh," replied Cloudy Quartz.

"Anyway, I only left him back at the farm

because he said he'd miss all of his rock buddies," Pinkie explained to her friends. She turned back to her parents. "Marble and Limey promised to look after him!"

Marble Pie's face remained blank. Limestone Pie blinked. *Plink, plink.*

Igneous cleared his throat and started to pace back and forth across the grass. "This here has got nothin' to do with pet rocks or parties, Pinkamena."

"Well…why are you guys in Ponyville, then, Dad? Huh? Huh? Huh?" Pinkie looked to the faces of her family but couldn't read them at all. "Oooh, let me guess! Are we going on a family vacation to Appleloosa? Or…I know, I know! You came to bring me some of Granny Pie's scrumptious rock cakes!" Pinkie looked around, but her family hadn't brought any satchels with them.

"No, that's not it.... Okay, okay, I give up! Tell meeeee!" Pinkie's eyes were practically popping out of her head with excitement.

"Your mother, sisters, and I are here for a very important reason," Igneous began. Pinkie frowned. Whatever it was, it didn't sound very fun at all. In fact, it sounded... *serious.*

"Well, word got 'round that you are friends with—" Igneous looked around nervously, realizing he had an audience of curious Ponyville residents watching his every move. "We heard that you might know..." Igneous puffed up his chest and finally announced, "We are here to see Her Royal Highness, Princess Twilight Sparkle, regarding a very urgent business matter!"

"We need to see the princess," Cloudy said. The sisters nodded in unison.

Pinkie's face dropped. "You're not here

to party *or* to see me?" She pouted, slumping down to the ground like a deflated balloon. "This is the worst surprise ever!"

"I'm sorry, but we have to talk to the princess and then get back to the farm right away," Cloudy replied. "We don't have time for any of this party nonsense right now."

"Oh, I see." Pinkie sighed.

"It's not nonsense!" Twilight said, stepping forward. "And I'm right here."

Everypony turned to look at Twilight, who up until now had been happily blending into the crowd. Usually, when she was at home in Ponyville, she preferred that everypony treat her like they did before she became a princess. None of this "Your Royal Highness" mumbo jumbo that every other pony in Equestria insisted on. Twilight still wasn't used to all the attention, but she would do anything to help a friend, and it seemed like Pinkie needed her to play the princess role today.

Twilight straightened and spoke in her most regal voice. "Welcome to our fair Ponyville." She bowed as she had seen Celestia and Cadance do.

Igneous, Cloudy, Marble, and Limestone immediately bowed their heads and leaned their front hooves on the grass to show their respect. "Princess!" Igneous Rock said, standing up again. "Thank you for having us. We'd be so grateful if you'd help us out."

"I'll help in any way that I can, Mr. Rock," Twilight said. Then she added, "Pinkie is, after all, one of my *very best friends*." Cloudy and the sisters looked down at their hooves, a little embarrassed for the way they'd just treated Pinkie in front of royalty.

"That's great news, Your Royal Highness," said Igneous, taking off his hat. But he didn't sound too chipper. In fact, despair was written all over his face. "It's great news...because we are about to lose the rock farm." The crowd gasped, even though most of them hadn't known the farm existed until then. It just seemed like the right response.

"What?!" Pinkie Pie shouted, practically leaping into the air.

"How dreadful!" exclaimed Rarity.

"Major bummer!" remarked Rainbow Dash.

"Oh, that's really too bad," whispered Fluttershy. "Those poor little rocks."

"Say, Pinkie, are you okay?" asked Applejack, giving her friend a sideways glance. "She looks a little...different, right?" she whispered to Rainbow Dash.

Pinkie did look strange all of a sudden. Her eyes were wide with terror, and she stood completely frozen to the spot. Fluttershy and Rarity exchanged concerned looks. Igneous Rock's news had been shocking to say the least, but they'd never seen Pinkie look so utterly...speechless.

"Somepony poke her or something!" said Rarity. "I've never seen her stand still before. It's so strange!"

Spike ran over and gave her a gentle nudge. "Uhhh, you okay, Pinkie?"

Pinkie looked up, her face full of sadness. "Everypony go home," she said, casting her eyes down at the ground. "This party is...over." Everypony gasped. Nopony ever expected to hear Pinkie Pie say such a thing.

CHAPTER 6

The Pink Sheep of the Family

★ ★ ★

Pinkie Pie had always been the silliest, most fun-loving pony in town. If she was that upset over the closing of a rock farm, then it must be a big deal. For the rest of the day, every-pony was abuzz with gossip and chatter about how Pinkie Pie herself had actually broken up a party! What was Equestria coming to?

"But I thought she didn't even *like* the rock farm!" Rarity whispered to Rainbow Dash. They were following Applejack as she led Pinkie's family over to the big barn at Sweet Apple Acres.

"Well, the rock farm was her home, so she's probably sad it will be gone," Fluttershy offered in her tiny, gentle voice. Her pink mane fell over one of her pretty blue eyes. "I can't imagine such a thing."

"I guess there's no place like *stones*?" Rainbow joked. "Okay, okay, I'll admit it— that was bad."

"Hey, are those emeralds around the flower border?" Rarity gasped, trotting up to the barn entrance. She was easily distracted by gemstones, no matter where they were. "How *divine*!"

"Come on inside, y'all," Applejack said,

ushering her friends and Pinkie's family inside.

"At least we'll have a li'l bit of privacy in here." She peeked her head out the barn door to make sure there were no stray party ponies following them. The Pie sisters looked at their surroundings in awe. Everything seemed to be so much brighter in Ponyville than back home.

"Good call, A.J. Now, where were we?" Twilight walked over and hugged Pinkie. Luckily, she had started to perk up after Apple Bloom brought her an Emergency Cupcake. Thank goodness Pinkie had recently installed a few pink glass cases around Ponyville for situations just like this one. A cupcake was an instant cheerer-upper.

"What happened to the farm, Mr. Rock? And what can *all of us* here in Ponyville do to help?" Twilight wanted to make sure the family understood just how important her friends were to her. Being a princess required lots of support. It wasn't just a one-pony job.

Igneous sat down on a wooden bench and hung his head. It looked like he had the weight of the whole rock farm on his shoulders. Marble, Limestone, and Cloudy Quartz trotted over and sat beside him. They all looked really sad.

"Go on now, Iggy," Cloudy said with her slight country twang. She patted her husband on the back. "Tell the princess here what's goin' on."

"Why don't you explain, Cloudy?" he said, looking tired.

"Yeah! Tell us, Mom!" Pinkie said, jumping up and down. She couldn't take the suspense any longer. "Tell us now!"

"Calm down, for granite's sake," Cloudy replied. "I'll tell ya!"

But before she could begin, Limestone blinked her eyes and cleared her throat. "It's the gems!" she blurted out.

"The gems?" Rarity asked. Any mention of jewels always piqued her interest. "What about them?"

"Ever since that Crystal Empire showed up again, all anypony wants are stones that shine, sparkle, and shimmer!" Cloudy explained. She cast her eyes down to the floor in defeat, and her bottom lip started to quiver. "Plain old rocks are boring."

"No, they're not, Mom!" Pinkie cut in. "Rocks are so totally awesome! There's slate!

And granite! And marble! And mudstone! And—"

"Well, you tell that to the rest of Equestria," Marble Pie replied. "We haven't had any business for months!"

"That's awful!" said Twilight. She felt especially bad, thinking of all she had done for the Crystal Empire. She never expected the rest of Equestria to be affected by its return, especially by turning ponies out of their homes.

Pinkie suddenly recalled that very morning when she'd seen Cheerilee's gem-lined front path. And Rarity had just pointed out that the Apple family had put in some gems around the barn. Now that Pinkie thought about it, it did seem like a lot of ponies right there in Ponyville were really into jewels lately. But Pinkie Pie never considered how that trend could be a problem for anypony, let alone her own family.

Pinkie looked at the sad faces of her two sisters and her parents. The gravity of the situation hit her like a ton of rocks. She had to do something, *anything*, to help them! Pinkie may have left her rock-farming days behind her, but the last thing she wanted was for her family to lose the farm. She pictured the old barn, the rock fields, and the drab gray landscape. It wasn't much, but it was home. *Thinkie, Pinkie!* she said to herself. She thought extra hard.

And then it came to her.

Pinkie began trotting around the barn, skipping and shouting. "I know! I know!" She did a grand leap and landed right in front of her parents. A puff of dirt and hay from the ground billowed up around her, and Limestone sneezed. "We'll throw a party!"

Pinkie Pie announced. "Then nopony will take you guys for granite anymore! Get it?! For *granite*!" She laughed.

Applejack and Rainbow Dash chuckled.

"A party?" asked Cloudy Quartz. She furrowed her brow in disapproval. "I don't know about that...."

"Yeah! But not just *any* party, Mom!" Pinkie said, growing more excited by the second. "A party dedicated to the total amazingness of rocks! It will be...a rock...a rock concert! We'll get bands and all sorts of rocks to decorate and invite everypony from every city all over Equestria to our very own PONY-PALOOZA!" Pinkie smiled wide and spread her arms as if to say "ta-da!"

Twilight, Rainbow Dash, Applejack, Fluttershy, and Rarity all turned to Pinkie's family for some sort of reaction. Marble frowned.

Limestone blinked. Cloudy winced. And Igneous remained stone-faced.

"What a splendid suggestion, Pinkie!" Rarity finally said, breaking the silence. "What do you think, Mr. Rock?"

"I think..." Igneous said, stepping forward. "That it's..."

Everypony leaned forward in anticipation of what he would say. "It's..."

Pinkie's smile grew with excitement.

"It's...the silliest idea I've ever heard in m' life! This is not something one of your parties can fix. Why can't you be serious for once, Pinkamena?"

"Well, I just thought that it could be super fun if—"

"Fun?" Igneous interrupted. "Why don't you go run along now and leave us alone with the princess so we can figure this out for real?"

Marble flipped her straight gray bangs, and nodded in agreement with her father.

Pinkie's face fell. All she'd wanted to do was help—and in the best way she knew how. And ever since she'd left the rock farm to live in Ponyville, parties had been her whole entire life. Pinkie Pie loved nothing more than to make other ponies smile. Usually, a little laughter and fun could ease even the worst problems!

It had even worked the day Pinkie had gotten her cutie mark. She'd thrown her very first party for the whole Pie family, and they'd all laughed and danced and smiled! So why wasn't it working now?

Pinkie looked to each of their faces. Nopony was smiling. Maybe they were right. Maybe she did need to stop being so silly all the time. Maybe it was time to be a little more serious.... If it meant that much to her family, then it meant that much to her. She made a decision right then and there.

"Mom, Dad," Pinkie Pie said, looking to her parents. "I, Pinkamena Diane Pie, *Pinkie Promise* to be a super-serious daughter from now on and not to throw any more parties! Cross my heart, hope to fly, stick a cupcake in my eye!"

Pinkie's friends looked at one another in shock. There was nothing in Equestria that would make Pinkie Pie break a Pinkie Promise! The situation with the rock farm had just gone from gravelly to grave.

CHAPTER 7

Pinkamena Serious Pie

★ ★ ★

As soon as Pinkie Pie woke up the next morning, she went straight to work on becoming the new Pinkie she had promised to be.

"No more messing around, Gummy!" she said to her pet alligator. "I'm Pinkamena *Serious* Pie now. Please don't bother me with any party invitations or fresh cupcake offers.

No swimming in the lake or dressing in silly costumes. All my time will henceforth be devoted to finding a super-duper serious way to save the rock farm!"

Pinkie trotted over to the mirror on the wall next to her Pinkie Party Planner and took a look at her reflection. Her hair had already fallen a little flat against her head, almost as straight as Marble's and Limestone's. But she still needed something else to look really serious.

Luckily, the mess she'd made the day before while trying to find a party inspiration still covered the floor. There were flags and party horns and costumes all over the place. Pinkie immediately spotted a great accessory for her new persona.

"These are perfect!" Pinkie said to herself, snapping the goofy fake nose and mustache off her favorite pair of joke glasses and popping the frames onto her face. "Now I look like I mean business."

Pinkie ripped down the Pinkie Party Planner and replaced it with a plain white calendar. It had lots of blank space to fill with important meetings and brainstorming sessions. "First on the Save the Farm schedule is to clean up this room! I can't have party hats and noisemakers distracting me if I am going to be thinking of really *serious* ways to save the farm." If she was going to focus, she couldn't be surrounded by such fun, colorful stuff! It all had to go. Pinkie got to work packing up all her party things in boxes. She didn't even bother to put each decoration and costume in the right place.

After Pinkie dragged the heavy boxes

down the Sugarcube Corner stairs, she got to work on the rest of the place. Pinkie had just started painting her room a drab shade of brown when she heard a hoof knocking on the door.

"Oooooh, a visitor!" Pinkie yelled out, forgetting to tone down her giddiness. "I'll be there in two shakes of a little lambie's tail!"

Pinkie dropped the paint roller into the pan, and it landed with a splat. Specks of brown paint splashed onto Gummy, who responded with his usual blink. Pinkie bounded to the door and flung it open.

Standing there was none other than Twilight Sparkle. She was wearing her princess crown, which was strange because she usually didn't unless she had to.

"Hellooooo, Twilight!" Pinkie sang out

with a singsongy lilt. She quickly realized that the greeting sounded far too excited and corrected herself. "I mean...ahem. Welcome, Ms. Sparkle. How may I help you this morning?" She tried to keep her voice monotone, like her sister Marble Pie. It wasn't *so*, so hard.

Twilight made a funny face. "So I guess you *were* serious about being serious, huh?" She stepped inside the room.

"Abso-tootley-lutely!" chirped Pinkie, then quickly added in her new voice. "I mean—yes, I am." She looked down at Twilight through her joke glasses.

"Why are you covered in chocolate, then?" Twilight asked, looking at the brown splotches all over Pinkie. Twilight didn't want to mention the odd glasses Pinkie was wearing. "Were you baking your famous double chocolate chip 'chipper' muffins again?" She hoped so. Twilight licked her lips just imagining the scrumptious taste of them. Pinkie was such a great baker.

"No, silly-willy Twilight!" Pinkie Pie said. "Look around! I'm redecorating! Or should I say... *undecorating*? Pinkamena Serious Pie would never have such a fun bedroom to play in. Once I fix all this stuff right up, finding a way to save the farm will be a piece of rock cake!"

"Undecorating?" Twilight said, suddenly noticing the blotchy brown paint all over the walls. What had Pinkie done? She loved her colorful bedroom! This situation was worse than Twilight thought. She had only ever seen Pinkie act this oddly one other time—when she and the gang had avoided going to Gummy's After-Birthday Party.

They'd only done it to plan a surprise party for Pinkie herself, but she'd gone all kooky. Pinkie had started talking to a sack of flour, some lint, a bowl of radishes, and a pile of rocks, claiming they were her best friends. This situation wasn't looking much better.

"Brown paint? No parties? Straight hair?" Twilight asked. "Pinkie, this isn't who you are! I came here to find you. We are going to plan the rock concert, just like you said! And we need your help."

"Thanks, but no thanks, Twilight!" Pinkie said, shaking her head. "You heard them.... My family isn't interested in any more of my little parties. So I have to find another way to save the farm."

Pinkie picked up the paint roller again and began to paint. Her glasses didn't fit quite right and kept sliding down her nose.

Whenever she pushed them back up, she smudged more paint on her face. It looked super silly, but Twilight couldn't even laugh. Her friend was in trouble!

Twilight trotted to the door, feeling defeated. "Well, Pinkie, I guess it looks like *I'm* going to plan a Ponypalooza rock concert. Let me know if you have any suggestions!"

Maybe, just maybe, if Twilight showed Pinkie how much the ponies needed her help with the party, she wouldn't be able to resist.

CHAPTER 8

Pinkie-less Party Planning

✳ ✳ ✳

It was unfortunate, but Twilight could already tell that Pinkie's family wasn't going to be much help, even though they'd finally agreed to let Twilight put on the show. Somehow, when they'd heard it from the princess's mouth, it seemed like a better idea than it had when Pinkie said it. But it was too late—they'd already hurt Pinkie's feelings, and now she was trying to be serious just to please them.

"All right, everypony. Let's put our brains together and try to figure out how exactly Pinkie Pie does this," Twilight Sparkle said to her friends. Twilight was surrounded by books on rocks, party planning, and rock music . . . but she had no idea where to start! Planning a rock concert was such a big task, and there wasn't much time. "Then we can figure out how to get Pinkie back to her normal silly self again."

Twilight picked up a purple book called *Geodes of Western Equestria* and began to read aloud. " 'A geode is a spherical stone that has a plain, rocklike appearance on the outside but on the inside contains a glittering, shiny center that consists of—' "

Rainbow Dash and Applejack exchanged a skeptical look.

"I'm sorry, Twi, but how is studying rock books going to help us plan a rock concert?" Rainbow Dash asked. Unless it was a Daring Do story, Rainbow didn't care too much for reading. "Shouldn't we be out there getting our hooves dirty?"

"Maybe we should try recruitin' some pony bands to perform at the show," offered Applejack. "I heard that Octavia might know the bassist from Nine Inch Tails."

"I could start on some decorations," said Fluttershy. "Or at least try to."

Twilight closed the book. "You ponies are right. This isn't getting us anywhere."

"Where are the Pie sisters? Surely, they have some opinions on the matter," Rarity said. "It is *their* party, after all!"

"I doubt it," answered Twilight as she began to use her magic to put away the stacks of books. Her horn sparkled, and the hardbacks floated gently up to their shelves, one by one. "If you haven't noticed, the Pies aren't too into parties. I only got the family to agree to let us put on the concert by telling them it was my official Royal Advice!"

"Where are they now?" asked Fluttershy, peeping out the window. "They looked so lost at the party yesterday."

Twilight nodded. "I completely agree. That's why Spike is giving them a tour of Ponyville. I told them that Spike was my Royal Tour Guide and it was a special honor to be shown around by him."

"They sure do look up to ya, huh?" Applejack said, pointing to Twilight's tiara. "Bein' a princess and all!"

"Now if only they'd believe me when I say the best pony for this job is Pinkie Pie!" exclaimed Twilight. "Then they'd see just how special she is to all of us here in Ponyville."

"Don't worry, Twi," said Rainbow Dash, looking smug. "Once we start putting the party together, Pinkie won't be able to help herself! I give her a few hours before she's in here calling all the shots."

Twilight looked down at her massive party to-do list. "Rainbow—you've just given me a great idea. I know exactly how to get Pinkie back!"

CHAPTER 9

Perusing Ponyville

★ ★ ★

"And this is where we all go to buy our quills and sofas," Spike told the visitors, standing in front of a little shop called Quills and Sofas. His presentation was met with little enthusiasm from Igneous Rock, who just stared back, chewing on a piece of hay.

"Is this where *the princess* buys her quills

and sofas?" Cloudy Quartz asked. Marble and Limestone listened intently.

"Yes, Twilight gets all her quills from here, too...." Spike groaned. Pinkie Pie's family certainly was starstruck by the idea of a royal pony in their midst. Every place they had visited, Cloudy had wanted to know Twilight's opinion on it. Marble and Limestone didn't say much; they just followed along. The two of them seemed to have an unspoken language that consisted mostly of blinks and nods.

"Does she send a lotta letters to Princess Celestia? To Canterlot?" Igneous questioned politely. "I've never been there m'self, but I hear it's real nice."

"Well, actually, I send the letters," Spike explained. "She tells me what to write, and I put it on the scrolls!"

"Is that so?" Igneous nodded his head and eyed Spike suspiciously as they continued. He still wasn't too used to hanging out with a talking baby dragon.

"I guess we can head to the Carousel Boutique next," Spike announced, leading the way. "Rarity owns it! She is known around Ponyville as the prettiest, um...I mean, most *fashionable* pony in town!" Spike still had a hard time containing his crush on Rarity. He blushed, but Pinkie's family didn't even notice. They had their sights on something else.

All of a sudden, Marble and Limestone gasped. Cloudy yelled out, "Iggy! Look at that over there!" They trotted over to Cheerilee's front walk and stared down at the glittering gems.

"This is what's puttin' us outta business!" Cloudy cried. "And I hate to admit it, but it does look *real* nice." The sisters crouched down to look at the jewels, much like Pinkie had done the day before. Cloudy started to cry. "We're doomed!"

Igneous hushed his wife. "Calm down, dear. We got a princess on our side now! She'll fix everythin' right up. Then we'll all be back to work on the rock farm before you know it."

Spike noticed Marble and Limestone Pie frown. They definitely looked like they could use a little less work and a little more play. Maybe they could come visit their sister more often and learn a thing or two about having fun. That is, if she ever switched back to normal....

"Oh, you're right, dear. Everythin's gonna be all right. Thank Celestia that Pinkamena is stayin' out of it like a good li'l filly," said

Cloudy, looking down at Igneous through her glasses. "You know how that girl gets an idea in her head and won't let it go."

"Mmmhmmm," Igneous Rock agreed, tipping his hat.

Spike felt bad for Pinkie. The way the whole family was treating her was ridiculous. She only wanted to help! And now she was driving herself bonkers trying to please them. Spike decided that the next stop on the tour had to be Sugarcube Corner. Maybe it would be just the thing to sweeten them up.

CHAPTER 10

A Visit to Sugarcube Corner

✶ ✶ ✶

Pinkie had just finished changing all her bedroom accessories from bright, bold colors to shades of brown and gray when she heard somepony outside. She trotted over to the window. Down below, she spied with her little Pinkie Eye—her family! They were with Spike, who appeared to be gesturing wildly at Sugarcube Corner.

"Hey! Hey, parents! Up heeeeere!" Pinkie was excited to show them how serious she could be. "Look up here!" Pinkie shouted again.

Finally, they caught a glimpse of their transformed daughter. With her stick-straight mane and the glasses on her face, she was starting to look more like them again.

"Pinkamena! What are you doing up there?" Igneous shouted. The piece of hay he was chewing bobbed up and down in his mouth as he spoke. Cloudy Quartz squinted up at the window.

"This is where I live, family! Come up and see!" Pinkie shouted. She turned to Gummy and giggled. "Oh goody, goody rock hops! This is going to be fun! I mean—it's going to be ... serious fun."

A moment later, Igneous, Cloudy, and Spike trotted inside the colorless room. Pinkie did a little twirl. "I *undecorated*! Just for you! Now I can be serious all the time!" Pinkie said, making a stern face. It didn't suit her.

"That's nice, dear. It's good to see you've made it look more like the barn back home. Is that Granny Pie's quilt over there?" Igneous pointed to the new blanket on Pinkie's bed—a gray-and-black creation with quilted rock shapes all over it.

"Oh yes," said Pinkie. "That's my basalt blankie, all right! Where are Marble and Limey? I want them to meet Gummy!"

"They are waiting downstairs, Pinkamena," her dad said, heading toward the door. "We don't have all day to just chat! We have business with the princess."

"Wait! You guys don't even want to hear my serious ideas to save the farm?" Pinkie said, looking crushed. "I have been thinking real hard all day!"

Cloudy patted Pinkie on the back before trotting out after her husband. "That's nice, dear. Tell us later on, ya hear?" Pinkie's shoulders slumped. Once again, Pinkie Pie had been unable to please her parents.

"Bye, Mom. Bye, Dad," Pinkie called out.

"Are you all right, Pinkie?" Spike asked, growing more concerned by the minute. "Are you sure you don't want to help Twilight and the girls with the party?"

There was a little glint in her eye, but it quickly passed. "I'm totally fine-eriffic, Spike. I'll just have to try harder! No parties! Pinkie never breaks a Pinkie Promise, remember, silly? Gotta go! See ya later, Spike!" Pinkie bounced out the door and down the stairs.

"Oh boy! That's what I was afraid of...." Spike said, looking at Gummy. "We gotta do something! Want to come with me to go find Twilight?" The little alligator blinked. "I'll take that as a yes!"

The Pinkie Trap

★ ★ ★

Rainbow Dash and Applejack stood in the middle of the road by Sugarcube Corner, waiting for Pinkie Pie to leave her house. "Are you sure this is going to work?" asked Applejack. She looked up at the big bunch of balloons she was holding in her hoof.

They looked pitiful. Every single one was misshapen or needed more helium.

"Are you kidding? Of course it will!" said Rainbow. "Look at these! There's no way Pinkie Pie will be able to stand how these balloons look. She'll want to show us how it's done. Then, she'll be reminded of how much she wants to help with the party and everything will be back to normal!" Rainbow pretended to brush some dust off her shoulder. "Easier than riding the Dizzitron at the Wonderbolt Academy."

"If you say so," Applejack said, craning her neck. They'd been standing there for quite a while. "I just hope we didn't miss her already."

"Miss who?" asked Pinkie Pie, who had somehow appeared right beside them. "Are you giving somepony a balloon surprise?"

Pinkie asked, struggling not to smile. She eyed the balloons hungrily.

"Well, not exactly…" Rainbow Dash said, playing along. "See…Applejack and I were just put in charge of balloons for the Pony-palooza party. How do these look, Pinkie? Perfect… *right*?" Rainbow paced around Pinkie like she was a royal guard interrogating a suspicious pony.

"Yeah, they're, um…" Pinkie started to sweat, and her eyes began to dart around. She looked at the balloons, desperate to say something. Her hair even started to puff up a little teensy bit. "They look just…"

"Yeah?" said Applejack. "How do they look?"

"They look guh-reat! Keep up the good work!" Pinkie said, regaining her focus. "No time to stay and chat! Serious business to take care of!"

Rainbow Dash and Applejack sunk down in defeat.

"Bye, Pinkie!" Rainbow called out, and then turned to Applejack. "I thought we had her for sure!"

"Don't worry. The others are ready to go," Applejack reminded her, watching Pinkie canter off into the distance.

As soon as Pinkie turned the corner by the Carousel Boutique, Rarity trotted outside to catch Pinkie. "Darling, I'm so glad I saw you passing by! I need your advice on these posters for the rock concert!" Rarity pulled out a large stack of hoof-made posters, covered in pictures of flowers and bows.

Pinkie scrunched up her nose. "They're nice and all, Rarity, but why the flowers and bows? It's a rock concert, silly!"

Rarity smiled. "Oh? Then what should I put on them?"

"Um...rock things?" Pinkie was using all her Pinkie Power not to explode into some sort of party monster right there. She was itching to take over, but she held fast to her promise to her family. "Actually, I think they are great just like that. Good luck with the posters, Rarity! See ya later!"

Rarity sighed as she watched her friend leave. "Well, I *tried*," she said to herself. "These posters are absolutely hideous!" She threw them up into the air, and they gently floated back down on top of her.

But Pinkie Pie was on a mission. She *needed* to get to the library. Little did Pinkie know, Twilight and some other guests were expecting her there, too.

CHAPTER 12

A Peace of Pie

★ ★ ★

As Pinkie made her way to Twilight's home at the Golden Oak Library, she thought about how she'd resisted helping Rainbow and Applejack with those poorly inflated balloons. And then she'd stopped herself from redesigning Rarity's posters, even though they'd made no sense at all. While she couldn't believe her own Pinkie Power, she felt a little funny—and not in a good way. Why had she given up parties again? Pinkie was starting to forget the reason. She found herself imagining the right way to blow up a balloon and what sort of rock concert poster would look really awesome.

Focus, Pinkie! she thought as the library came into view. *You have to save the farm!* All she needed were a couple books, and Twilight just had to have them. Twilight was really smart, after all, and books were where she found most of her answers.

"Knock, knock, Twilight!" Pinkie shouted into the window. "I really, really, really, really need some books!"

"Come on in, Pinkie!" Twilight shouted from inside. "What sorts of things are you looking for?"

"Well, I'd like one on growing cucumbers and then one on how to run a rock circus and maybe a—" Pinkie pushed open the door, expecting to see just Twilight and Spike. Instead, she saw them—plus Rarity, Applejack, Rainbow Dash, Fluttershy, *and* Pinkie's whole family!

"Is this a surprise party?" Pinkie asked, her glasses sliding down her nose again. "Because I'm tooooootally surprised!" Pinkie started to smile and then looked at her family and remembered why she had come there in the first place. "I mean, not that I like parties. I hate parties! *Blech*, parties are the worst thing ever!"

"You know that's not true, Pinkie Pie," said Twilight.

"Of course it is! I'm Pinkamena Serious Pie—the most serious-est pony in all of

Ponyville. Maybe even Equestria! Would anyone like to schedule a business meeting with me?" Pinkie pulled out a planner and pen and started scribbling furiously in it.

"No, but we would sure like our old friend Pinkie back," Applejack said, stepping forward. Rarity, Fluttershy, and Rainbow nodded in agreement.

"And we'd like our Pinkamena back, too," Igneous Rock said, joining them. He looked a little embarrassed, but he was smiling.

"You…you would?" Pinkie couldn't believe her ears. "But I thought…I thought that my parties were too silly for you! I thought you wanted me to be serious!"

"We're so sorry, Pinkamena, dear," Cloudy Quartz said. "We didn't mean to hurt your feelins'. We've just been under so much stress about losin' the farm and, well…we didn't think you'd understand. You've always had such a sunny outlook on things!"

"But I do understand! I do!" Pinkie said, taking off her glasses. "All I wanted to do was help!"

"We see that now, thanks to Princess Twi—thanks to all your *friends* here," said Igneous. "You're a real lucky pony. They were the ones who told us how you'd changed yerself just to please us. This talking baby dragon here was real concerned." Spike puffed out his chest.

"Well, Gummy and I were both worried," admitted Spike, patting the alligator on the head.

"We didn't realize what we had done until we saw you out the window just now, struggling to hold back your natural talent and not helping your friends."

Cloudy shook her head. "You don't need to do that ever again, sugar! We love you just as you are."

"Oh, family!" Pinkie felt herself bubbling over with happiness. She ran over to her family and scooped up all four of them in a big hug. "You guys are the bestie-westest!" When she pulled away from the embrace, her mane was at maximum poof. Pinkie Pie was back!

"Now that *that's* all over, we just have one question for you, Pinkie...." her mom said.

"What is it?!" Pinkie shouted, bouncing up and down. "Ask me! Ask me! Ask meeee!"

Igneous Rock cleared his throat. "Will you plan our rock concert party?"

Pinkie pretended to think about it. "Oh, all right. If you really want me to!"

Everypony cheered. Now they were really back in business.

CHAPTER 13

Pinkie Takes Action!

★ ★ ★

Pinkie snapped straight into action. It was all hooves on deck to rescue the party, and Pinkie could not have been happier. She bounced around the room, speaking a million words a minute. Her family stood by, amazed. Their eyes followed Pinkie as she darted back and forth, giving orders to everypony in the room. She was like a pin-ball in an arcade game.

"Rainbow Dash, you're in charge of the invitations! I'll need hundreds of tiny bags of rock candy with equally tiny parachutes on them! You can talk to Mrs. Cake about the candy and to Davenport at Quills and Sofas for the parachutes. Did you know he also does custom printing?! Little-known secret for those in the know. You and the other Pegasi take them all over Equestria! GO!" Rainbow nodded and rushed out the door.

Pinkie's mane was getting fluffier with each second. "Fluttershy, you call your old pal Photo Finish and tell her to bring in some of her famous friends! Spread the word that we need the biggest and rockingest bands in all of Equestria to perform! I want

every musician we know up on that stage—
Octavia! Lyra Heartstrings! DJ Pon-3! Lyrica
Lilac! Neigh-Z! Don't worry, though. I *also*
have some secret connections if those ponies
fall through!"

Pinkie winked at Twilight, who just looked
baffled. Nopony knew that Pinkie had celeb-
rity friends. But she was full of surprises.

"Got it," Fluttershy said softly, and trotted out the door in a hurry.

"Applejack! Mom!" Pinkie shouted. "You're
next!"

"Me?" said Cloudy Quartz, looking around
as if there were some sort of mix-up.

"Totally!" Pinkie laughed. "You guys are
in charge of TREATS! I want apples. I want
rock cakes. I want apple rock cakes! Enough
to feed all of Equestria! Go, go, go!"

Applejack saluted Pinkie and led a very

confused Cloudy out of the cottage. "Come on, Mrs. Quartz! This is gonna be fun! We can go on a bakin' spree at Sweet Apple Acres!"

"Rarity! Twilight! Marble Pie! Limestone Pie!" Pinkie called out. The four ponies stepped forward, ready to receive their orders. "You ponies are in charge of… DECORATIONS!" Marble and Limestone exchanged an excited smile, finally allowing themselves a little fun. Their sister's enthusiasm was catching on!

"Oooh! That's just the job I wanted!" Rarity said, clapping her hooves together. "Okay, girls, I have so many ideas for the main stage curtains! I'm thinking velvet, maybe some gray satin? Black, shiny ropes and some marble columns? Going with sort of a rock-stone-chic look, you know?"

"That sounds amaaaaaazing!" Pinkie squealed. "The more rocks, the better!"

"Got it, Pinkie!" said Twilight, nodding. "Whatever you want!"

There was only one pony left without an assignment. Igneous Rock shuffled his hooves in the corner. "What should I do, Pinkamena?"

"Dad!" Pinkie bounced over to him. "You have the most important job of all!"

"I do?" he said, looking at his jubilant daughter. "What is it?"

Pinkie jumped into the air. "Have fuuu-uuun, of course!" she yelled before trotting out the door. "This totally rocks!"

CHAPTER 14

Pinkie Pie in the Sky

★ ★ ★

The roads to Ponyville were soon jammed with crowds of ponies from all over Equestria trying to make their way to the concert. The skies were busy with Pegasus traffic, and the Friendship Express train was at full capacity. It seemed like all of ponydom had come out for the party!

Pinkie watched in awe from high up in the sky. She was in Twilight's balloon, shouting greetings to the sea of ponies below and sprinkling them with rock-shaped confetti. "Welcome, everypony!" she yelled into her megaphone. "Welcome to PONYPALOOZA! You're all going to have the rockingest time EVER!" This was the biggest party she'd ever planned. It was so thrilling!

"Yaaay, Ponypalooza!" Fluttershy yelled quietly, flying beside Pinkie. Her voice was too soft for extreme cheering, but she tried her best. She landed inside the basket of the balloon and turned to Pinkie. "What a great turnout for the concert! You ready for your big entrance?"

They had the whole thing planned out. Pinkie would land onstage, thank the guests for coming, and tell them about the rock farm. Then the concert would begin, and everypony would rock the night away!

"You betcha-wetcha, Fluttershy!" Pinkie yelled into her megaphone. It was so loud that it caused Fluttershy's pink hair to blow backward in a gust of wind. Fluttershy winced. "Whoopsies!" Pinkie giggled, moving the megaphone away from her face. "Sorry, got a little *carried* away!"

"It's okay!" Fluttershy said, taking off again. "I'll see you down there soon, Pinkie!"

A few moments later, Fluttershy arrived at the front entrance. It was decorated with several large rock piles, bunches of rock-shaped balloons, and a festive banner. Twilight and the others were there, wearing their all-access badges. Pinkie Pie's family stood beside them, watching as the hordes of eager attendees entered the field. There was a buzz in the air, and it wasn't just the happy bees that were flitting around in the fragrant flowers.

"This is going to be sweet!" a tall royal-blue stallion yelled to his pack of buddies. "I can't believe Pinkie Pie got Coldhay to perform! They are totally my favorite band of all time!"

"Yeah, and I heard they are going to do a set with the Whooves," said his beefy red stallion friend with a guitar cutie mark. "It will go down in Equestria history as the most rad performance ever!"

Just after them, a group of giggling mares wearing matching shirts all trotted inside. "When does John Mare go on? I'm so in love with him."

Igneous Rock's eyes were wide with disbelief. "How did our little Pinkamena do all this? I've never seen so many ponies in my whole life!"

Igneous turned to his wife, who also looked shocked. Cloudy's jaw was practically on the ground. "And they all came out to help us?"

"What did I tell you?" Twilight smiled knowingly. "You have a very special daughter. She sure knows how to bring ponies together." Twilight turned to Rarity and whispered under her breath, "Now, let's just hope it works!"

"Oh, it will, darling," said Rarity, winking. She was full of giddiness and excitement herself. For a social butterfly like Rarity, this was heaven. "It will!"

The two ponies hoof-bumped and ran off to their assigned stations. It was almost time to get this rock party started!

CHAPTER 15

The Rockin' Ponypalooza Party!

★ ★ ★

Just inside the front entrance, Applejack was working the cider and apple rock cake booth. "Come get 'em! Apple rock cakes! Pie family secret recipe!" she hollered to the crowds. She really didn't need to try very hard to sell them. Cloudy Quartz had helped her with the recipe, and the cakes were delicious. So far, the concertgoers were buying them faster than Applejack could dish them out! They'd already sold two whole batches, and the show hadn't even started yet. "Giddyup, Apple Bloom! Bring out another batch!"

"Got it, sis!" the little filly replied with an excited smile, and ran off to do as she was told. Sweetie Belle and Scootaloo followed her. "We'll help, too!"

Near the stage, Rainbow Dash was pumping up the crowd with some awesome Wonderbolt-style tricks. She dived into a barrel roll and flew right above the hundreds of ponies. Then she landed on the stage and hoof-bumped a white pony with a blue streaked mane and sunglasses. It was none other than DJ Pon-3, who was busy spinning some beats to get the party started on her turntable.

Suddenly, a couple of Coldhay's road-ponies burst through the crowd and ran toward the stage.

"Go for Casper!" a white stallion in a headset shouted, and was quickly followed by a young Pegasus doing the same. "Go for Razzi! T minus three minutes to showtime! Let's go, everypony!" Whispers of excitement rippled through the crowd, and everypony stamped their hooves on the ground.

The sun was just starting to set over Ponyville as Pinkie Pie's balloon floated down onto the stage. DJ Pon-3 transitioned to a new song as Pinkie hopped out of the basket.

"Fillies and gentlecolts of Equestria!" Pinkie Pie shouted into her megaphone. "I'm Pinkie Pie, and I'm here to welcome you to...the first annual Pinkie Pie Family Rock Farm Ponypalooza Party!" The ponies went wild with cheers. Pinkie bounced and flipped all over the stage. "Let me ask you this: Do you love rocks?! I know I do!" Pinkie screamed into the megaphone. The crowd started chanting *rock* over and over. "Wahooooooo! Are you ready to rock?!"

"Yeah!" the crowd yelled back.

"All right, let's goooooo! Please welcome Canterlot's very own...COLDHAY!!!!" Pinkie Pie welcomed the band and waved to the crowd as she exited.

By the end of the night, it was Pinkie's name that the ponies were all chanting. It was the most fun she'd ever had—because she was being herself and nopony else. It rocked.

CHAPTER 16

A Rockin' Success

★ ★ ★

Over the next few days, all anypony could talk about was the rockin' success of the Pinkie Pie Family Rock Farm Ponypalooza concert. The performances had been stellar; the ponies had danced all night. And most important of all, they were reminded of how totally awesome rocks were!

It was incredible how the rock farm had gone from struggling to thriving overnight. Igneous and Cloudy were taking orders for front path stones, cottage bricks, and even pet rocks! It seemed like everypony wanted something! Cloudy and Igneous couldn't *stop* smiling.

When it was time for them to go home, Pinkie Pie and her friends gathered to wish them a safe journey. "How can we ever thank you, Pinkie?" Igneous Rock said to his daughter. Cloudy and Pinkie's sisters stood nearby with wide smiles on their faces. "You saved the farm!"

"I could never have done it without the help of my friends...and you guys!" Pinkie giggled. "Wasn't it a fantilly-astically great time?!"

"Abso-tootley-lutely!" answered her dad

with a wink. "Be sure to come and visit us on the farm, now! Your mother's birthday is coming up real soon."

"A birthday?!" Pinkie's eyes grew wide and she did a little kick. "You know what that calls for?"

"A party!!" everypony chorused.

"Hey! How'd you guys know what I was gonna say?!" said Pinkie Pie.

CHAPTER 1

The Latest and Greatest
★ ★ ★

It was almost midnight in Ponyville, but nopony was tucked into bed yet. They all had the same very good reason for staying up past their bedtime: There were only four measly minutes to go until it was *time*. Time for the most epic adventure ever to be released— *Daring Do and the Volcano of Destiny*!

"Omigosh, omigosh, omigosh!" said Rainbow Dash, a blue Pegasus pony with a rainbow-colored mane. She bit her lip and began to pace around the patch of grass outside the Ponyville bookshop. Even though she would have the precious book in her hooves in less time than it took for her friend Pinkie Pie to throw together a party (her current record is four minutes, seventeen seconds), Rainbow Dash still felt so fizzy with anticipation that she thought she just might explode. As awesome as a rainbow firework would look, however, Rainbow didn't have time for it. Not now. Not on the release night of the most incredible adventure book *ever*! Plus, if she exploded, she'd lose her place in line.

Three more minutes, she thought. Hardly any time at all! Yet it seemed like an eternity for the biggest fan of Daring Do in all of Equestria.

"Can't you ponies hurry it up in there?!" Rainbow whined as she peered through the window of the bookshop. "I *need* that book right now!" The light was on and there was some movement inside, but the CLOSED sign had not been flipped around to OPEN just yet. Giant posters of Daring Do adorned the shop windows. They showed the famous adventurer Pegasus wearing her signature outfit—a khaki pith helmet and an olive green shirt. On the new book cover she was shown standing at the mouth of a volcano bubbling with fiery red lava. The words above bore the book's title: *Daring Do and the Volcano of Destiny.* Below the cover, the poster read MIDNIGHT RELEASE PARTY! GET YOUR COPY BEFORE EVERYPONY ELSE!

Rainbow snickered as she glanced at the large crowd behind her. It had grown a ton in the past few hours. It looked like two hundred ponies were there. Thank Celestia, she was first in line! Nopony else loved Daring Do as much as Rainbow Dash did. To prove it, she'd been camping out since the morning. She brought all of the Daring Do books with her and had spent the day rereading them so she could have the stories extra-fresh in her mind. When midnight struck, she wouldn't have to wait a single tick of the clock longer to find out what happened to Daring next. It. Was. Going. To. Rock!

The Daring Do series of books had become extremely popular lately, and Rainbow Dash suspected it was mostly because of her. After all, she was a major trendsetter in Ponyville. Other ponies looked to her for anything extremely awesome or cool. So it was only natural that the bookshop had decided to make it a special event. It had closed early in the afternoon to prepare for the festivities. Some of the ponies in line wore homemade Daring Do costumes, and some munched on goodies from Applejack's treat cart. But they all had one thing in common—they were beyond excited to continue reading about Daring Do and her thrilling adventures.

"Get yer Apple Fritters...of Destiny!" Applejack said, trotting up and down the line with a tray of treats for sale. "Fresh Caramel Apples...of Doom?"

"Hey, Applejack?" Rainbow asked her friend. They just looked like normal treats to her. "Uh...what are you doing?"

"Figured I'd try to make my treats from

Sweet Apple Acres sound as Daring Do as I could," Applejack explained. She picked up a mini apple pie and passed it to Rainbow. "Apple Pie of Fate? It's my last one!"

"Thanks, but no," Rainbow said, pushing the treat away. "It's almost time!"

Plot Twist, the yellow Earth pony with an orange mane who owned the bookshop, poked her head out of the door to count the ponies in line. "So many readers!" she observed with delight. It was fun to see so many young fillies and colts interested in reading.

"We're almost ready, everypony!" Plot Twist shouted at the line. She was glad she had recruited Pinkie Pie to help her with the party. They had expected a large crowd, but nothing like this. She needed all the help she could get.

"Oh, man!" Rainbow squirmed. "This is taking for-ev-er!"

"Hiya, Rainbow Dash!" Pinkie Pie chirped, poking her bushy fuchsia mane out of the window. "Are you, like, so totally excited that you feel like you're going to burst into a rainbow firework of happiness and super bubbly joy now that you're going to get the new Daring Do book first?! Are you?! Are you?!"

"Exactly!" Rainbow nodded. "Now, can we get this show on the road? I have a story to read! I just have to know what happens with Dr. Caballeron! Is the Volcano of Destiny his secret lair? Or is it just a decoy to distract Daring from finding the Secret Stables of Crickhowell?" With each word, Rainbow inched closer to Pinkie's face like she was interrogating her.

Pinkie shrugged and smiled wide. "I don't know, but it won't be long before you do! We're just putting the finishing touches on the replica of Ahuizotl's temple we made. It's built completely from books! Isn't that totally readeriffic?!" Her eyes sparkled with delight.

"Yeah, yeah. Very cool. But hurry it up!" Rainbow said, jogging in place. She'd been waiting outside for a long time. Her legs and wings were starting to majorly cramp up. And since she'd been waiting alone, she hadn't even had one chance for a flying break.

Rainbow had tried to get her friends to come, but none of them had wanted to wait all day long. Fluttershy and Rarity had stopped to visit but had to go tend to some newborn goats and finish sewing hats for them, respectively. Twilight Sparkle loved Daring Do, too (she was the one who'd originally introduced the series to Rainbow Dash), but she had decided to wait until her copy arrived in the mail the next morning. She mumbled some nonsense about needing sleep so she could get up early to do some studying before her Daring Do book arrived. She said reading would "distract her," so she'd better get her work done first.

It was so silly! What could be more important than this?! At least Applejack and Pinkie Pie were there, even if they were both working.

"Only one minute left, everypony!" Rainbow Dash shouted to the line. Her call was met with cheers. The sound of the crowd triggered something inside of her.

Hundreds of ponies watching? Excited fans? One minute left? It was more than enough time to make a grand entrance into the bookshop! If she flew at the door at just the right angle...yeah, she could do this. She would do it for Daring Do!

Rainbow Dash turned to Applejack's big brother, Big McIntosh, who was in line behind her. He was wearing a Daring Do helmet and chewing on a piece of hay. She'd have to trust him to keep her place. "Watch my spot, Big Mac!" Rainbow shouted.

"Eeeyup," he said, nodding his light orange mane.

"Hey, Daring Do fans! Watch *THIS*!" Rainbow hollered. The ponies all started chattering. What crazy thing was Rainbow Dash going to do now? The store was about to open!

Rainbow bolted into the air, beating her blue wings as hard as she could. She shot off into the distance, a rainbow trailing behind her that was so bright it was visible in the night sky. It happened so fast that if a pony had blinked they would have missed it.

"Hey, where'd she go?" asked Apple Bloom, pointing to the sky. "I don't see her anywhere!"

"There she is!" squeaked Sweetie Belle in her little filly voice. "She's headed straight for the door!"

Up in the sky, Rainbow Dash could see the sign on the door flip from CLOSED to OPEN. The door was still closed, but if she'd calculated the timing correctly, everything would work out perfectly. She'd be the first to get the book and she'd do it with style.

"Daring Do, here I coooooome!" Rainbow

shouted as she completed a perfect triple barrel roll across the sky, leaving a corkscrew rainbow in her wake. Rainbow Dash swooped down like a kamikaze pilot. Everypony in line held their breath. She was getting dangerously close to the shop! Would she crash into the door? Apple Bloom and Sweetie Belle shielded their eyes with their hooves.

Several ponies gasped as Rainbow hurtled herself forward, about to make contact. Then, at the very last second, the door opened!

"Iiiiincomiiiiiiing!" Rainbow Dash hollered as she dived through, narrowly missing Plot Twist, who had come to greet the eager fans.

Bang! Boom! Crash!

When the dust had settled, all that was left

of the grand towering replica of Ahuizotl's temple was a big pile of books with a rainbow Pegasus in the middle. Even though Rainbow's stunt had ruined the display, it was a good thing the books had been there to soften the landing. At least that's what Rainbow told herself as she looked around at the destruction. Sometimes it took a little sacrifice to do something impressive, so the trade-off was totally worth it. Plot Twist frowned. Clearly she didn't agree.

"My display is ruined!" Plot Twist cried, throwing her hooves in the air.

Rainbow gave a weak laugh as she stood up, books falling off of her. "Whoops, sorry about that. I know it looked great." Then Rainbow snatched up a book, dropped her bits on the counter, and took off for Cloudsdale to read through the night.

CHAPTER 2

Patience IS an ISSue

★ ★ ★

"And then what about the part where Daring swooped through the massive barricade the henchponies had constructed?! I couldn't believe she made it! Even though they were blocking the path to the secret stone that unlocked the hidden gates that led to the road to the Volcano of Destiny!" Rainbow Dash yelled.

She spread her blue wings out wide in excitement. Her voice was so loud that anypony within a mile radius of Ponyville Park could have heard her. The only other times she got this worked up was when she was flying, performing a Sonic Rainboom, or when she saw one of the Wonderbolts do a sweet new trick.

"Spoiler alert! La, la, la...!" Twilight sang as she held her hooves over her ears. She shook her head back and forth in protest.

"Uh, Twilight? What are you doing?" asked Rainbow Dash, raising a skeptical eyebrow. "Don't you want to talk about how so totally awesome the book is?! Especially the part where—?"

"No!" Twilight yelled. She softened her

tone and added, "Sorry. I mean, no. No spoilers, *please*?"

"You're not finished yet?!" Rainbow whined, doing a dramatic twirl before falling to the ground. "This is the worst! I thought *you* of all the ponies in Equestria would be done reading it by now! Don't eggheads like you just, like, *look* at books and absorb what's in them, anyway?" She groaned.

Twilight smirked. Sometimes Rainbow said things that sounded harsh but were really compliments in disguise. Whenever she called Twilight an *egghead*, she really meant that she thought Twilight was smart.

"Well, I *can* speed-read, but this is a book I really want to savor and enjoy." Twilight held up her copy. "A new one of these doesn't come out every day, you know."

Of course Rainbow knew! She'd only been waiting for this Daring Do adventure for what—*months*?

"Hey! What is that and why didn't I get one?" Rainbow pointed to the Daring Do bookmark stuck in between the pages, about a third of the way through. It was shaped like the famous relic from the first book in the series, the Sapphire Stone. It was actually pretty sweet.

"They sell them at the bookshop. You can have this one if you want," offered Twilight. She passed it to Rainbow, clearly trying to make up for her disappointment.

"Nah, it's okay," Rainbow said, handing back the bookmark. It was a nice gesture, but Rainbow Dash's number one problem still wasn't solved. She needed to find some- pony who had finished reading the book so she could go over all the new awesome stuff that had happened in the story! *Now*. "How am I supposed to talk about the coolest parts of the story if nopony has finished yet?" Rainbow groaned.

"Sorry, Rainbow," Twilight said, taking a seat on her favorite bench on the perimeter of Ponyville Park. "But I'm going to take my time." Then she opened her book and got settled for a slow, relaxed reading session.

"I guess reading is just another thing that showcases how fast I am and how slow everypony else is," Rainbow Dash mumbled before taking off into the clouds. "Story of my life."

Fluttershy, who was leading a group of ducklings to the pond at Ponyville Park, happened to walk past just as Rainbow Dash took off. Fluttershy noticed the look of dismay on Twilight Sparkle's face, so she made a detour. "Hold it right there, little sweeties," the yellow Pegasus cooed to her feathered followers. "I'll be just an itty-bitty moment, and then we'll go for that little paddle like I promised." The ducklings responded with tiny, happy quacks.

"Hi, Fluttershy," Twilight said, still looking to the sky in concern. Up in the sky, Rainbow kicked a cloud in frustration. It disappeared with a poof. She frowned and looked for another puffy cumulus to take her anger out on.

"Is something wrong with Rainbow Dash?" Fluttershy asked, looking toward the sky. "She seems...a little down."

"She wants to talk about the new Daring Do book, but nopony's finished reading it yet," explained Twilight. She furrowed her brow in concern.

"Oh, I just started reading it," said Fluttershy. "But I had to put it down to take care of my daily duckling duties. It's quite good so far!"

"I just wish there was something we could do to help her. It's so great to see a pony so excited about reading." Twilight sighed. "If I had it my way, everypony would read all the time! Then, we'd have meetings and discuss what we'd learned and exchange ideas."

"So why don't you do that?" asked Fluttershy. "It seems like fun!"

"Fluttershy, that's perfect!" Twilight replied, standing up. "We'll plan a Daring Do book club, and we can hold it at the library. Then Rainbow can talk about the books all she wants!"

Rainbow flew down so fast that Fluttershy and Twilight didn't even see her coming. "Now THAT'S what I'm talking about!" she cheered as she did a little backflip. "By the way, I was totally listening to your whole conversation."

CHAPTER 3

The Golden Oak Library Society
★ ★ ★

A few unbearably long days later, Rainbow Dash's wish was about to come true. Book Club Night! It would be nothing but talking about Daring Do all evening! By the time Rainbow arrived, Twilight Sparkle's home was already bursting at the branches with ponies who had recently finished reading

Daring Do and the Volcano of Destiny. Everypony had come prepared for the very first meeting of the newly established Golden Oak Library Society. One by one, they filed into the library clutching their copies of the book and chattering excitedly about its contents. Rainbow Dash took a seat at the front and watched the room fill up. This was going to be awesome.

Plot Twist and Berry Punch walked in together, followed by their friends Lyra Heartstrings, Sweetie Drops, and Wild Fire. They all poured themselves cups of cider from Applejack's refreshments table and took their seats.

"Daring Do is such an exciting hero! I just love her!" said Berry Punch.

"This was the best book yet!" said Plot

Twist. "We completely sold out in the first hour at the shop."

Sweetie Drops nodded in agreement. "The next book release will have to be even bigger."

"Totally," Wild Fire added, her voice monotone. The brown-maned pony wore straight-edged bangs that hung over her eyes and a chilled-out expression. It was still the most excited she had ever looked. Pinkie Pie popped up out of nowhere. "Name tags, anypony?!" She passed each attendee a little red sticker that said: HELLO, I'M…_____. Pinkie was already wearing one, except instead of her own name, she'd written HELLO, I'M…<u>EXCITED</u>!

"You're *Excited*?" asked Sweetie Drops. The pony scratched her blue-and-pink mane in confusion.

"Sure am!" Pinkie replied with a smile. "Aren't you?!"

"I'm confused," Sweetie Drops replied. She already knew Pinkie Pie. "You're—"

"And I'm excited you're here, *Confused*!" said Pinkie, passing her and Lyra some name tags. The two ponies shrugged at each other.

"Sorry I'm late, darlings! I wasn't sure what one wears to a library society," announced Rarity, waltzing in the door. "But I managed to rustle something up." She was decked out in a collegiate ensemble, consisting of a sweater over a collared shirt and horn-rimmed glasses. Her saddlebag was filled with quills and notebooks. She definitely could have passed for a student at Mythica University. "I never tried the bookish look, but I think it really works on me, no?"

"I think you look great, Rarity!" said Spike, popping his head out from the other room.

Before Rainbow Dash could add her two bits on Rarity's look, Fluttershy stepped inside. A little green inchworm followed her. He was wearing glasses and a tiny Daring Do pith helmet. He scooted in, moving almost slower than Tank, Rainbow Dash's pet tortoise. "I hope it's okay that I brought my friend William Wormsworth," she said in her gentle tone. "He's a bookworm. He loves books ever so much and begged to come along." William smiled and scooted to the top of a stack of Daring Do books.

"Of course," said Rainbow anxiously.

"And it's nice to meet ya, Will. But please sit down now so we can get on with it!" It felt like everypony moved slow on purpose to frustrate her. Where was the hustle?!

But still, Rainbow was happy to see that all her friends had shown up for the meeting. The discussion was bound to get really heated and not just because they were going to talk about the Volcano of Destiny. She was going to impress everypony with her new theory. Rainbow was pretty sure that the Volcano of Destiny would become the Hollow Hideout of the prophesied Stalwart Stallion of Neighples in the next book. Surely, nopony else had made the connection between the newly recovered ancient map of the underground fortress of Mount Vehoovius in chapter four and its similarity to the one mentioned in *Daring Do and the*

Griffon's Goblet. It had to be the same one! She just knew it.

"All right, everypony. Find a seat and we'll get started!" Twilight announced. There was a twinkle in her eye. Clearly, anticipating a whole evening of talking about books with her friends had brought her to almost the same level of enthusiasm as Rainbow Dash.

Twilight had certainly worked hard to make the event very official. The room was arranged so that the ponies could sit in a semicircle. It was a little bit like a classroom but more casual. The book-lined walls of the hollowed-out tree set the mood nicely. A big chalkboard listed the order of business for the meeting.

"Welcome!" Twilight chirped. "I'm so glad you're all here to share in the joy of reading with me! In my opinion, there are not enough events in Equestria purely for celebrating books, especially the Daring Do series!"

For once, Rainbow Dash wholeheartedly agreed. She didn't even care if it made her an egghead.

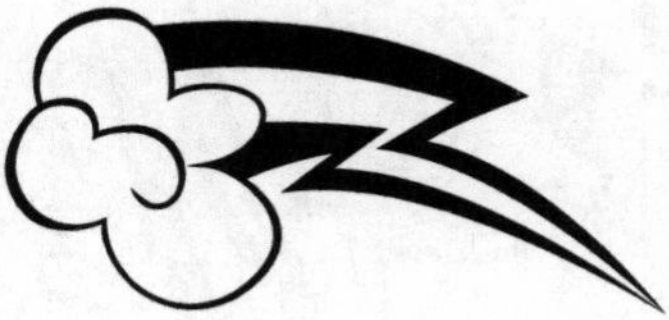

CHAPTER 4

The Double Dare

★ ★ ★

Pinkie Pie squirmed in her seat next to Rainbow Dash like she was sitting in a pile of ants, except she had a huge grin on her face.

"Oh my goodness, Rainbow! You must be so thrilled! I mean, Daring Do is, like, your favoritest pony character ever, and we're about to spend *hours* talking about her! What are you thinking right now? What are you feeeeeeling?" Pinkie leaned in until she was about an inch from Rainbow's face.

"I'm thinking I want to talk about Daring Do and I'm feeling annoyed that we aren't yet," Rainbow deadpanned.

"Great, great. Okay, that's great." Pinkie nodded as she scribbled something on a notepad. "And how does *that* make you feel?" She propped her chin on her hoof.

"Pinkie Pie!" scolded Twilight. "We're starting! Shhhh."

"Consider my lips zippified!" Pinkie procured a zipper out of thin air and taped it to her mouth.

"So…" Twilight motioned to her blackboard, which was filled with tons of writing and diagrams. "I've done some extensive research into how to run a book club meeting," she explained excitedly. "Number one on the agenda should be introductions of each member of the group."

"I think we all know each other already!" Rainbow shot back. "Moving on!"

"Nuh-uh!" said Pinkie Pie, the zipper falling off her mouth. She pointed to Sweetie Drops. "Have you all met *Confused* yet?!" Sweetie Drops shook her head in defeat.

Twilight ignored the exchange. "Okaaay, so if we skip that part…next should be a quick recap of each chapter in the book to refresh everypony's memory. Then, we'll move on to general interpretations of the text and its meaning, and last we'll go through the list of discussion questions. We'll have one ten-minute snack break in the middle, so please wait to visit Apple-jack's treat table until then."

Rainbow Dash looked around the room. A quick survey of the skeptical faces confirmed that she wasn't the only one who didn't think Twilight's schedule sounded all that fun. Rarity was busy inspecting her new hooficure, Sweetie Drops was staring out the window, and Lyra Heartstrings was slouching down in her chair with her hind hooves dangling in front of her. She looked indifferent.

Rainbow jumped in before things got worse. "I think I speak for everypony here when I say we can cut straight to discussing the ridiculously sweet action sequences." Plot Twist nodded her wavy orange mane in agreement.

Applejack interjected, trying to be a bit more gentle, "I think what she means is maybe we should giddyup on gettin' this thing goin'."

Twilight had the best of intentions, but sometimes she was an overplanner. And right now she looked pretty disappointed that her Library Society agenda hadn't gone over so well.

Fluttershy felt bad. She raised a hoof and said, "Twilight, if it's okay with you, William Wormsworth and I would love to stay after and discuss all your talking points. He usually has a lot to say, the little chatterbox!" William sat on his chair, smiling but not saying a peep. He hadn't said a single word yet. He tipped his pith helmet to Twilight like a gentleman.

"It's all right." Twilight sighed. "Rainbow Dash, maybe you should take over." Twilight found an empty seat. She was a good friend for trying, but Rainbow was more than happy to take the reins of this meeting. Now they might actually get somewhere.

"First things first: I can't believe that move Daring Do did where she hitched a ride on the back of that dragon and let go right when she was over the middle of Ahuizotl's encampment! I can't wait to try that out sometime! Of course, I'll need help finding a dragon...."

"At your service!" said Spike proudly. It was silly because he was still just a baby—and far too small to pull off a stunt like that. It was better to change the subject before he got his feelings hurt.

"Riiight." Rainbow clapped her hooves together. "Anywaaaay, how about I tell you all my amazing and totally brilliant theory on the ancient map of Mount Vehoovius?!"

This was her moment to wow them. "So, you know how in book two—on page one hundred sixty-three, to be precise—Daring Do is looking for the griffon's goblet when she happens upon a tablet that refers to an ancient map? I think that—"

Wild Fire raised her hoof, interrupting Rainbow's flow. "Um, excuse me?"

"Yeah?" Rainbow replied, trying to hide her annoyance. She didn't like being interrupted. Especially when she was about to say something so epic that it was going to blow everypony's minds.

"I like Daring Do as much as the next pony, but do you *really* think that all those daring things she does are *realistic*?" Wild Fire flipped through her copy of the book, frowning. "No way could a pony ever really do them in real life!"

"She has a point," said Lyra. She nodded and bobbed her mint green mane.

"Some of it is pretty far-fetched," added a blue Unicorn seated in the back. A couple of other ponies murmured in agreement.

"Like the part where her wing injury is acting up, so she has to step out onto an invisible rope bridge to cross the canyon?" said Sweetie Drops, flipping to the page of the scene in her book. "No way would anypony risk that."

They were clearly missing the point of a fun adventure story. Twilight chimed in with a serious counterpoint. "I don't think the purpose of the books is to—"

"Are you guys kidding me?!" Rainbow shrieked, interrupting Twilight. Her eyes grew as wide as a couple of Granny Smith's prized giant zap apples. "Of course, all the stuff she does could be real! Daring Do is the bravest pony ever. I wouldn't be surprised if she *were* real!" Rainbow puffed up with pride.

Twilight, Applejack, Rarity, Fluttershy, and Pinkie Pie each shot Rainbow a warning look. If she wasn't careful, she was going to say too much.

"I guess I'd just have to see it to believe it, is all," Wild Fire said, giving a little shrug.

"Well...maybe you can," Rainbow Dash said, walking up to Wild Fire. The expression on Rainbow's face was a familiar one—determination. She'd looked the same when she saved Rarity by performing a Double Rainboom in the Cloudsdale Best Young Flyer competition. Just like nothing would have gotten in the way of saving her friend from falling then, nothing was going to stop her from proving her point now.

"Oh yeah?" replied Wild Fire, standing up to challenge her. "And just how are you going to do that?"

Applejack stood up and positioned herself between the two ponies. "All right now, everypony, why don't y'all just slow yer trot for a second? This is just a book club."

Rainbow Dash and Wild Fire stared at each other. Even though things were getting heated, it was a friendly challenge.

"Oooooh, I sense a dare coming on! This meeting is already way more exciting than I expected it to be!" Pinkie Pie said, jumping up and down. "And I was already excited." She pointed to her name tag. "See?"

Rainbow turned to the rest of the ponies

in the room. She climbed on top of a chair for dramatic effect. "I...I *dare* anypony here to dare me to do anything Daring Do could do!" She put her hooves on her hips in triumph.

"And I...dare you to do so!" replied Wild Fire. She narrowed her eyes. "No—I *double* dare you!"

Everypony gasped. To Rainbow Dash, a dare was unbreakable. But a double dare? That was a whole new crate of apples.

"Called it," said Pinkie.

CHAPTER 5

The Daring
Dash-Board

★ ★ ★

The next day, there was a big stir in the Ponyville town square. Everypony was gathered around the center, trying to catch a peek at something. Pinkie Pie had taken the lead in helping Rainbow Dash carry out her dares.

Pinkie Pie stood proudly next to a giant

rainbow-colored scoreboard, making grand motions with her hooves and urging ponies to come up and write their challenges on it. The frame was surrounded in decorative glittery clouds made of cotton balls and said DARING DASH-BOARD in bubble letters at the top. The proud expressions on the faces of the Cutie Mark Crusaders—Apple Bloom, Scootaloo, and Sweetie Belle—were dead giveaways as to who had helped make it. Those three little fillies loved arts-and-crafts projects. Their teacher, Cheerilee, who had many hoof-made cards from them at home, could vouch for that.

Rainbow Dash trotted up and waited for the ponies to start showering her with words of praise and adoration. But they were all so busy admiring the Dash-Board that they hadn't even noticed the guest of honor had arrived! Rainbow cleared her throat loudly to get their attention. "Umm, guys? Bravest pony in Ponyville present. You can all chill out now, because I'm here." She turned her nose up to the sky and closed her eyes.

"Oh wow, it's Rainbow Dash!" shouted a small green Unicorn filly, jumping up and down in glee. "Is she really going to do whatever anypony dares her to do?"

"She's here! She's here!" shouted Scootaloo. She was Rainbow Dash's number one fan; a rainbow-colored hat was pulled down over her short pink mane. "Come on, Rainbow!"

"Or you can all go wild," said Rainbow nonchalantly. "That's cool with me, too."

Everypony watched as Rainbow Dash parted the crowd with her confident trot and took her place next to Pinkie Pie.

Rainbow now saw that the board had a bunch of lines where ponies could write their names and dares, and a spot for a check mark if Rainbow completed the dare successfully. Even though she hadn't read any of the dares yet, Rainbow had no doubt that every row would have a check mark next to it soon. She was fearless, after all. Just like her hero, Daring Do!

"Thanks for coming!" Rainbow shouted to the crowd. "I'm pretty pumped to see you all see me do some awesome stuff!" She took notice of Twilight, Rarity, Fluttershy, and Applejack entering the town square. They all had funny looks on their faces. What was the big deal? She was just trying to prove how brave she was.

"Pssst, Pinkie, will you do the honors of reading the first dare?" whispered Rainbow Dash. "It looks cooler if I have an assistant."

"Sure thing, Rainbow!" Pinkie chirped, and then faced the crowd. "Fillies and gentlecolts! The amazing *Daaaaaring Dash* will now take on all these extremely difficult challenges to prove that her hero Daring *Do* could also *do* these dares that she will *do*!" Pinkie made a grand sweeping motion toward the Dash-Board. "Then she will defend her title as Ponyville's very own most brave, most fearless, most DARING pony!"

The townsponies cheered. Rainbow smirked.

"Daring Dash's first dare is…"—Pinkie paused for effect—"to cross the Ghastly Gorge…"

Rainbow rolled her eyes. That was hardly a challenge. If she was going to make her point, these ponies needed to get a little more creative than that.

"...on a tightrope..."—Pinkie continued, making a dramatic face—"without using WINGS! Over the lair of the quarray eels!"

"All right!" Rainbow shouted, flying up into the air. "Now that's more like it! Everypony follow me to the gorge!" Rainbow shot off into the blue sky, leading the way. The crowd dutifully followed, trotting below. Would Rainbow chicken out and use her wings? Or would she make a misstep and risk falling into the jaws of a giant, scary quarray eel?!

Twilight, Applejack, and Fluttershy followed but stuck to the back of the herd.

"Is this all really necessary?" Twilight asked her friends, walking at an easy pace. "We all already know how brave Rainbow

Dash is, but sometimes she takes it a little too far." Twilight thought of the time Rainbow had become boastful after saving some townsponies and becoming a local hero. Her friends had devised a plan to remind her to keep her hooves on the ground and be modest. Clearly, that lesson was beginning to wear off.

"Don't you fret, sugarcube!" assured Applejack. She trotted alongside Twilight. "I reckon she'll do a coupla dares and it'll all be over in two shakes of a filly's tail. Now come on!"

Rarity trotted up to join them. "Well, if anypony understands the allure of attention, it's me. But somepony ought to tell her that if she's going to be famous, she should look the part. A costume would really add a certain something."

"Rarity, I don't think that would do much to discourage the whole thing," scolded Twilight.

"I was just *saying*," Rarity huffed. "Besides, it doesn't look like she's giving up her new persona anytime soon."

Up front, Rainbow was doubling back through the crowd, hoof-bumping any-pony she passed. She did a corkscrew flip and flew to the front of the group. "Ghastly Gorge, watch out!"

"It looks like she's having fun," said Flut-tershy, walking alongside her friends. "I just hope she's careful."

"Me too, Fluttershy," said the concerned Twilight. She watched as Rainbow dived straight toward the ground. At the very last second she did a one-eighty and flew up into the sky, full speed ahead. "Me too."

CHAPTER 6

Heating up
★ ★ ★

It had been a busy day for Rainbow Dash and the ponies who had been following her daring escapades. They'd been all over Ponyville and back again, watching as Dash took on a multitude of crazy challenges. Some were totally thrilling—like when Snips and Snails had dared her to swim to the bottom of the disgusting swamp, Froggy Bottom Bogg. Rainbow had gotten completely covered in green slime and gook, but everypony had been impressed.

Others were not quite *as* exciting—like Pinkie's dare for Rainbow to babysit her favorite yellow balloon for an hour. ("So many things could happen if he's left alone! It's very risky," she'd insisted.) But still, Rainbow Dash had completed each and every task, no matter the level of difficulty.

Rainbow took off into the air and felt the cool rush of the wind in her mane. "What else ya got for me?!" she shouted to the ponies below.

There was only about an hour left of daylight before Princess Luna would be lowering the moon over Equestria. But that was more than enough time to get a few more dares in. Rainbow Dash's friends had been following her all day, but as the hours wore on, they were getting more and more worried. She'd proved her point; why didn't Rainbow just put an end to the madness already?

"What was it you said again?" Twilight turned to Applejack. "Just a few dares and she'll be done? Look at her—she's been doing daring things like Daring Do all day!"

Applejack shrugged. "Maybe we can try a different approach to get her to give it up." She trotted up to Pinkie and whispered something in her ear. Pinkie nodded and scribbled a new dare on the board.

Rainbow Dash landed and trotted to the middle of the dwindling crowd, nose turned up to the sky. "Pinkie Pie, let's go over all the amazing feats I have completed so far."

"Oooh, fun idea!" Pinkie said, turning to the Daring Dash–Board. She pointed to each item with a long, glittery wand. "First, you tightrope-walked across quarray eel dwellings at Ghastly Gorge with no wings." The crowd murmured their approval.

"Piece of apple cake!" said Rainbow, hoof-bumping a nearby stallion.

"Then, you went inside the scary, old abandoned barn filled with bats...." Pinkie touched her pointer to the dare.

"I wasn't scared for a single second!" Rainbow assured her fans. "If anything, those bats were afraid of *me*."

"Awww," said Fluttershy, thinking of the poor little bats. "I hope they're okay."

"Then..." Pinkie took a long, deep

breath and then said very fast, "...you swam in the bogg, babysat my balloon, spun around in a circle two hundred times until you were totally dizzy, gave Rarity's kitty-cat, Opal, a bath, knocked on Cranky Doodle Donkey's door during his bridge game, performed a Sonic Rainboom through the tree obstacle course at Sweet Apple Acres, and now you're about to eat the hottest chili peppers in all of Equestria!"

"Woo-hoo!" Rainbow smiled, satisfied with her success. Then the last part registered. "Wait—did you say something about chili peppers?" Rainbow disliked hot peppers more than any other food in existence. And there was only one pony she'd told that secret to: Applejack!

"Yeah, she sure did," said the yellow country pony, stepping forward. "Peppers from South Amareica. I just got some down at the Fillydelphia market last week when I was making my pie deliveries. The pony who sold 'em to me carried them across the San Palomino Desert. He said a couple of those guys around the orchard would keep out pesky pests," Applejack explained. She leaned in close to Rainbow Dash and looked her straight in the eyes. "He also said that one lil' bite of one of 'em would make fire shoot straight out yer ears."

"TO THE BARN!" shouted Pinkie Pie, bouncing up and down. "Let's get the fire peppers!"

"But…but…" Rainbow Dash began to protest. Beads of sweat started to form on her forehead. What had she signed up for? "I don't like—"

"Yeeeeah?" said Applejack, giving a little wink to her friends. Twilight looked hopeful. Maybe her plan to get Rainbow to quit all this darepony stuff might just work. There was no way Rainbow Dash would ever eat a chili pepper.

Rainbow looked around at her audience. Suddenly their faces seemed to be bearing down on her. It was like they knew she was about to be defeated by some tiny, little, itty-bitty hot peppers. But that couldn't happen! Not now, after she'd done all that other stuff. To quit now would totally disprove her point.

"What I *meant* was…" Rainbow forced herself to stand a little taller. "I don't like how long you're taking to give me those peppers!" She smiled nervously and looked around. That seemed to satisfy the onlookers.

"What?!" replied Applejack. "Are you sure? Well, color me surprised and call me Golden Russet!" Applejack felt a little silly now that her plan was literally going to backfire.

"She's gonna do it!" A yellow Pegasus with a blue mane shouted.

"Go, Rainbow!" added Sweetie Drops. "Rain-bow! Rain-bow!" she chanted. It wasn't long before the whole crowd was egging her on.

"That didn't go quite as planned," Applejack admitted to Twilight, stifling a nervous laugh. Apparently, Rainbow Dash was on a roll, and she wasn't going to cool it for just anything. Not even a hot, hot pepper.

★ ✳ ★

As soon as Rainbow Dash bit into the pepper, all sorts of weird things started to happen. First, she felt like her mouth was on fire. Then, she could have sworn she saw Daring Do herself in the crowd. Finally, her ears began to feel hot and she heard the booming laughter of Ahuizotl telling her she could never defeat him. It was kind of awesome, in a way.

Rainbow coughed, and a few multicolored flames burst out.

"Look at that!" Spike laughed, clapping his claws together. "Rainbow can send all the letters to Princess Celestia now!" He found it particularly funny, since he was the only one who could breathe fire, as well as use its magic to deliver messages across Equestria.

"All right, now. That's it. Drink up, sugarcube!" Applejack patted Rainbow Dash on the back. She had insisted on bringing Rainbow an endless supply of water and cider to calm her tongue. She obviously felt very guilty about challenging Rainbow. Her plan had gone up in smoke.

"Thanks," said Rainbow, taking a big gulp. Everything seemed almost normal again, other than the fact that her tongue was now 20% cooler.

"I've never seen anything like that." Fluttershy shook her head in disbelief.

"Your face turned as red as an apple!" added Applejack.

"I'd say it was more of a deep crimson hue," said Rarity. "But it was dreadful."

"What about those rainbow flames that were shooting out of your ears?!" Pinkie squealed. "That was so awesometastic!"

"Was it?" Rainbow groaned, sipping

from her cup. "At least it impressed every-pony, because those peppers were brutal!"

Twilight gave Rainbow a stern look. "That's just what we're worried about. Your daring ways are starting to put you in danger!"

Rarity, Fluttershy, and Applejack all looked at Rainbow in concern. Pinkie slumped down with the realization that she'd been encouraging her all along.

"What?" Rainbow Dash took another sip of cider. "I'm totally good. And plus, I thrive on danger. Rainbow 'Danger' Dash! Now let me go back outside and greet my fans."

"Rainbow, my dear," Rarity chimed in. "I think what she's *trying* to say is that nopony expects you to be as brave as Daring Do. Maybe you should just focus on being Rainbow Dash. Hmm?" Rarity batted her long eyelashes and swished her purple mane. Unfortunately, her charm was lost on Rainbow, who was now standing up and brushing herself off.

"Uhh, as nice as that is, guys, I think I'll just stick to being the bravest pony in town and being the best." Rainbow trotted to the door. "But thanks for all the cider! Now I'm ready for even more action."

"I liked this whole Daring Do thing better when it was just about reading books," said Twilight with a sigh. Rainbow Dash could have used that Sapphire Stone bookmark right about now. She was starting to lose track of her place.

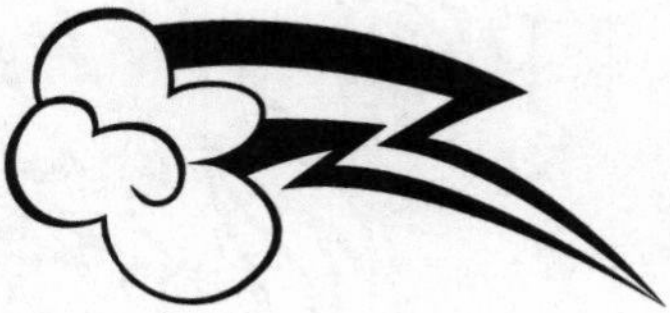

CHAPTER 7

The Talk of the Town
★ ★ ★

The next morning, Rainbow Dash awoke to the sound of a loud thunderclap. She popped her head out the window of her home in Cloudsdale. All the other Pegasi were darting around in a tizzy and jumping on the thick, gray clouds to drain them.

With each push, big raindrops began to fall on the landscape below. It was pouring!

"That's funny," said Rainbow Dash, still a little groggy. "I don't remember a heavy thunderstorm being scheduled for today." Usually, Rainbow Dash knew when all the weather changes were supposed to happen. But today, she was distracted and out of the loop.

Glitter Dew, a purple Pegasus with a blue mane and a starry cloud for a cutie mark, heard her and flew over. "We changed the schedule yesterday, but nopony could find you!" She darted off to join the efforts. "It's only a morning rainfall."

"What was I doing yesterday that was so important that I'd miss the weather schedule?" asked Rainbow Dash, scratching her head. Her brain felt a bit fuzzy. She'd had a weird dream about walking on a tightrope and then eating some insanely hot peppers. Unless...that was real! Rainbow touched her hoof to her mouth. Her tongue still felt a little numb. *Oh my gosh!* she thought.

The events of the previous day came flooding back to her. "That was no dream— that *is* what I was doing!" she said aloud. Rainbow Dash had spent all day zipping around Ponyville, showing everypony in town that she was the bravest pony ever. Now, she was known as Daring Dash— undeniably, unquestionably...unstoppable! "Great job, me!" she said, patting herself on the back with her right wing.

Suddenly, Rainbow Dash couldn't wait a single second longer to get down to Ponyville to greet everypony, especially her friends. Even though Twilight, Applejack,

Rarity, and Fluttershy had been totally skeptical before, there was no way they wouldn't have come to their senses by now. They'd have to admit that she kicked serious flank on those dares and nothing bad had happened! They really could be such a group of worry-ponies. All Rainbow Dash had to do now was sit back and wait for their apologies. And in the meantime, she would enjoy the praise that came with the title of being Ponyville's bravest.

"Sorry, guys," Rainbow shouted to the other Pegasi. "I've got somewhere to be!" Rainbow stretched her blue wings and smoothed down her multicolored mane. She gave herself a quick wink in the mirror and took off for Ponyville below.

Rainbow soared down from the sky and

immediately noticed how full the town square looked. Apparently, word of Daring Dash's amazing feats had been spread across Ponyville by Wild Fire. There were twice as many fans as yesterday. They all gathered excitedly, chattering and recapping their favorite dares. Some of them were even wearing their Daring Do costumes from the book party, but had added rainbow-colored wigs to the look.

Wow, thought Rainbow. *There sure are a lot of ponies here to see me.*

"Are you all excited for Daring Dash?!" Pinkie Pie shouted to the herd. She was standing on the platform in front of the Dash-Board. Her outfit of choice was a rainbow-colored "Daring Dash" T-shirt and a hat that looked like a giant hot chili pepper.

A few other ponies were wearing them, too, so there must have been a merchandise booth somewhere.

For some strange reason, Rainbow was starting to feel a little bit panicked. It was confusing. The scene certainly had a ton of things she loved—a crowd cheering her name, her best friends watching, and new, thrilling challenges to take on. Maybe it would be better to keep her entrance low-key this time. She landed in an alleyway and crept onto the scene, unnoticed.

A few more ponies trotted up, and Rainbow quickly darted behind a shop to listen to the conversation.

"I'm gonna dare Daring Dash to hoof-wrestle with Snowflake—the strongest Pegasus in Cloudsdale!" said a pink pony with a curly teal mane.

"Well, I'm gonna dare her to fight a manticore!" added an orange Unicorn with a cutie mark of a cactus. "With her bare hooves!"

"How about daring her to get a hooficure?" suggested their purple Earth Pony pal with a giggle. Rainbow cringed. She didn't like the sound of that one. If there was anything Rainbow hated more than chili peppers, it was beauty treatments at the Ponyville Day Spa.

"Ooooh, a hooficure?!" whispered Pinkie into Rainbow's ear. "How are you going to do that, Rainbow? You hate the Ponyville Day Spa!"

"Whoa! Where'd you come from?" shouted Rainbow, jumping back in shock and landing in the town square. Rainbow looked up at the platform in confusion.

Sometimes Pinkie Pie seemed to move faster than Rainbow! Pinkie shrugged.

"Is something wrong?" said Fluttershy, floating down to meet the two of them. "You seem a little jumpy today, Rainbow Dash."

"Of course not!" Rainbow shot back in defense. "Everything is perfect! Look at this place. Everypony loves me!" She took off toward the stage, leaving a rainbow trail behind her. But as soon as she landed, a large mass of dark clouds began to drift over the town square. Then a bright shock of light zigzagged across the sky. Rain poured down and began to drench the ponies.

"Aw, come on, guys!" Rainbow shouted up at the sky. "Couldn't you wait just a little longer to do that? We are sort of in the middle of something here."

"Sorry, Rainbow Dash!" Silverstream,

a gray Pegasus with a blue mane, shouted. "Carry on!"

"Thank you!" she shouted back, satisfied. Even the Pegasi did what she said.

Finally the clouds parted, and a strong ray of sunlight pierced through onto the crowd. One spot in the square was immediately lit up, drawing everypony's attention.

Standing in the middle was none other than Zecora—Ponyville's resident shaman! She wore lots of gold necklaces and a set of shimmering hoops in her ears. Her left foreleg was adorned with shiny bangles and she wore her black-and-white-striped mane short.

"What's up, Zecora?" said Rainbow Dash casually. In truth, she was a little nervous about the worried look on Zecora's face, but Rainbow couldn't let anypony see that.

Zecora did have a taste for the dramatic, and the whole clouds parting, personal-spotlight business had not helped the situation. Maybe whatever Zecora had to say would be no big deal.

"Citizens of Ponyville!" she bellowed in her rich, deep voice. Zecora paused, like she was struggling to find the strength to carry on.

"Is everything okay?" Twilight stepped forward, her voice doing little to hide her alarm.

Zecora continued, "I've come to summon the pony who has proved bravest..."

"Oh, well, in that case, I think you're looking for me. Bravest pony in town right here." Rainbow pointed to herself and puffed up with pride.

"...for only she can be the one to save us!"

On the other hoof, maybe it *was* time to panic.

Zecora's gold hoop earrings glistened as she nodded her head. "Of course, Rainbow Dash should be the one! Her skills and courage are second to none."

The zebra made her way toward the platform. A few ponies jumped out of the way, scared. It was silly. Rainbow Dash and her friends knew that Zecora wasn't actually an evil enchantress like they'd originally thought. She may have been lots of things—mystical, magical, and mysterious—but malicious was definitely not one of them. Too bad some stubborn ponies still held on to that fear.

"Anything you need, Daring Dash will do," Rainbow assured her with a salute. "So ... uh, what is it I'm doing?"

Zecora looked around at the group of ponies, her blue eyes full of worry. "A token that provides us protection was stolen for another's collection."

"Okay," Rainbow Dash nodded. "So you're saying it's pretty important and stuff. Got it. What is it?"

"The precious relic of a golden hue resembles the hook of a horse's shoe." Zecora waved her hoof toward the crowd, and a three-dimensional image of the relic appeared out of wispy green smoke. It spun around slowly in the air so that everypony could see it. One side of the horseshoe was completely gold, and the reverse looked rusted and beat-up.

Twilight Sparkle gasped and stepped forward. "You couldn't possibly mean . . . the Half-Gilded Horseshoe?!"

Rainbow Dash looked around to see if anypony else knew what Twilight was talking about, but their faces were all blank. Twilight knew a lot about a wide range of topics from all her studies on magical history.

"The what?" Applejack cocked her head to the side.

"Did she just say something about *gilded* shoes?" Rarity trilled. "Now you've got my attention!" She trotted up to the rotating image of the horseshoe and started fussing over it every time she saw the gold side. Rarity couldn't help herself around anything shiny.

"It's not *really* a shoe, it's...it's—the Half-Gilded Horseshoe is like a key of sorts. To the Spirit Circle," Twilight explained. "The myth says that the pony who unlocks it will find a room full of treasures, but at a great cost."

"Treasures?" asked Spike, his eyes sparkling. "Like gems? Big ones?"

"Maybe...but nopony really knows," said Twilight. "Honestly, I really thought the whole thing was an old pony's tale."

"Much of the legend is a mystery, and most regard it as ancient history," said Zecora. "But, I have failed as the key's protector, and so must prepare to face these specters."

"Am I missing something here?" Rainbow Dash asked. "An old rusty shoe was stolen and now somepony's gonna score some treasure." She lifted an eyebrow skeptically. "And this puts us in danger how exactly?"

Zecora swatted away the green smoke with her hoof. "The ghosts will be free when key meets lock. If you want to save Ponyville, fly fast, don't walk!"

Rainbow wasn't too sure about legends or ghosts, but if there was one thing she knew, it was flying fast. Rainbow stepped forward without another thought. "I'll do it!"

The shaman sighed and patted Rainbow on the shoulder. "It is a great relief that our best flyer will be the one to put out this fire."

"You bet! Never fear, Ponyville. Daring Dash is here!" she shouted, flying up into the sky. Finally, Daring Dash had her own real book-worthy adventure to star in. All that other stuff had just been practice.

Well Suited

★ ★ ★

The carousel boutique was an absolute mess. Swatches of green fabric lay on every surface, and pieces of thread and ribbons littered the floor. Half-drunk cups of tea sat on the sewing table. But it was crunch time.

Rarity paced around Rainbow Dash,

deep in concentration. "Stretch your left wing out again, please. And stop moving around so much." Rainbow sighed and did as she was told. Standing still was the absolute worst.

"I don't see why you need to add anything to it," groaned Rainbow. "My Daring Do costume from Nightmare Night is totally fine as it is! In fact, I can't wait to wear this baby on my quest to recover the Half-Gilded Horseshoe." She looked at herself in the full-length mirror. With her green shirt and pith helmet on, Rainbow was the spitting image of her hero. Well, almost.

"Because I *insist*," Rarity said, measuring the shirt again. "If you're not going to let any of us go with you, you have to at least let your friends help you prepare for your journey. You are seriously lacking in utility pockets." Rarity shook her head, shuddering. "Now *there's* a sentence I never thought I would say!"

"You know, Rainbow," Applejack chimed in. "You can still change your mind about the whole thing. We'll all be ready to go with you in a jiffy—just say the word."

Fluttershy, Pinkie Pie, and Twilight nodded.

"Yeah! It'll be like a party!" Pinkie Pie added. "But instead of streamers and balloons, there will be scary beasts and spiky hedges!" Pinkie stood up and waved her arms around like she was trying to scare them. "And I'll bring cupcakes. There's always room for cupcakes."

"Thanks, guys," Rainbow replied. "But if I'm going to maintain my image as the fastest and bravest, I can't have a bunch of other ponies slowing me down. Nothing personal."

"Well, in that case, we better go over all my research on the Spirit Circle." Twilight used her horn to magically carry over a large stack of books. They landed in front of Rainbow with a thud. "I think you'll be interested in what I discovered."

✶ ✶ ✶

"So let me get this straight—" said Rainbow. She was looking through one of the Daring Do books, hoping to memorize some more cool moves. "The entrance to the Spirit Circle can be found by…"

Twilight sighed. They had been over this a few times already. She was trying to make sure Rainbow knew everything that Twilight had found regarding the Spirit Circle, but the Pegasus wasn't making it easy. "By the Dual Stronghold—whatever that is—and is only visible once every five seasons... on the seventh day of the... third week of the year."

"That's so random," Rainbow said coolly, flipping a page in her book.

"It's tomorrow!" Twilight shouted, pointing to the calendar on her wall. "It's likely that whoever took the Half-Gilded Horseshoe will be there, waiting for the entrance to appear."

"Well, I'll be ready with the move that Daring Do used in the final scene of book four—the old switch 'n' fly. This is going to be totally easy!" Rainbow said, conjuring up an image in her mind.

She pictured herself getting to the

entrance of the Spirit Circle just in the nick of time. Then she would distract the Half-Gilded Horseshoe thief with an awesome stunt, snatch the relic by switching it with an item of equal weight and size, and then zoom off into the sky to return it safely to Zecora all before it was time for dinner. She would be miles above the thief by the time he noticed what had happened. No problem.

"Rainbow, don't forget the most important part," warned Twilight. "If whoever took the Half-Gilded Horseshoe opens the entrance, the spirits will get out!"

"Yeah, yeah," Rainbow Dash replied. She was already thinking of her homecoming party. Maybe Mayor Mare would give her a medal.

Twilight came up close to Rainbow Dash

and tried to look her in the eye. "And if they do, they will be freed for another whole season. You have to make sure the entrance is closed! Don't let the spirits out!"

"Yeah, yeah...got it..." Rainbow answered mindlessly. "Closed and stuff. It's all good." But, unfortunately, Rainbow Dash's head was still in the clouds.

CHAPTER 9

Enter the Everfree

* * *

The six ponies, Zecora, and Spike all stood at the clearing that led to the Everfree Forest. Rainbow Dash was wearing her new costume that, thanks to Rarity, had a ton of new pockets and a new, matching lightweight saddlebag. A picture of her cutie mark—a cloud with a rainbow lightning bolt—was embroidered on the collar of her shirt, and the fabric on her helmet was rainbow-colored. She certainly looked the part. Now it was all up to her.

"You sure you don't want company?" asked Applejack. "I feel mighty funny sending you out there alone." The six of them had been to the Everfree Forest more times than Applejack had liked, but at least they'd been together. It was a spooky and unpredictable place.

"For the last time, *no*," Rainbow answered. "Being the bravest means you don't need any help."

"Everypony needs help sometimes," offered Fluttershy.

"I know I do," Applejack insisted. "Remember that time I tried to buck all the trees in Sweet Apple Acres on my own?"

Zecora bowed her head. "It is time, Rainbow Dash, and I hope you are ready. May your wing beats be strong and your hoof beats be steady."

"Thanks. And don't you worry, Zecora," said Rainbow. She patted the pocket Rarity had added for the relic. "I'll have the Half-Gilded Horseshoe back in no time. No ghosts will haunt Ponyville if Daring Dash has anything to say about it." Rainbow twisted into an action pose—right arm up to the sky, wings spread out.

Zecora looked slightly reassured.

Rainbow Dash gulped and took a step forward. "See ya later, everypony."

"Wait!" shouted Twilight Sparkle. "We didn't even get to show you your tools yet."

"My what?" answered Rainbow, growing impatient.

"Each of those dreadfully practical new pockets has a little something from one of us to help you on your way," explained Rarity, smiling warmly. "Go ahead and look."

Sure enough, Rainbow Dash emptied the pockets to find a piece of rope from Applejack, a mini teddy bear from Fluttershy, some green cupcakes (and one pink one) obviously from Pinkie Pie, a pair of horseshoes from Rarity, and a Sapphire Stone bookmark from Twilight. They were the weirdest group of adventure "tools" she'd ever seen. Rainbow Dash wasn't sure how any of these things was going to help her, but her friends looked so proud. It was a nice gesture, so Rainbow played along.

"I told you there was always room for cupcakes!" squealed Pinkie Pie. "The pink one's for you."

"Thanks," said Rainbow, who was already planning to ditch the items as soon as she was out of their sight. No need to have anything extra weighing her down—that went for extra ponies *and* random gifts. She stuffed the presents back into her pockets. "Now I'm off for real!" Rainbow announced. Then she flapped her wings and soared straight toward her destiny.

As soon as Rainbow Dash was out of sight, Twilight turned to the other girls. "Are you all ready to go?"

"Yes!" Applejack, Fluttershy, Rarity, and Pinkie Pie said together.

Zecora bowed to them and Spike gave a little wave. "Be careful out there! Good luck!" the dragon said as the five ponies trotted toward the dangerous forest. He was pretty sure they were going to need it.

CHAPTER 10

In the Thick of It

✶ ✶ ✶

Rainbow Dash took a deep breath as she flew off. The humid air filled her lungs. It was a hot day, and the sun hung low in the sky. The gentle light illuminated every rock, tree, and bramble on the edge of the Everfree Forest. It was serene, but it was a false sense of calm. In a second, Rainbow would be deep inside it—the most wild, unpredictable place in all of Equestria. Other than Pinkie Pie's head, of course.

Mysterious bugs trilled and exotic birds cried out from the treetops. They seemed almost like they were saying "Do Not Enter!" but there was no way Daring Dash was going to heed the warning. She was the bravest pony in town. And she was on a mission to save Ponyville. Now where to start?

Rainbow Dash looked around and surveyed her options.

There was no visible path up ahead. Every direction was dense with green foliage that seemed to fade into black. It looked so...dark and cold. Rainbow Dash shuddered but then quickly shook off her doubt. "I can *totally* do this. I'm Daring Dash!" she said out loud to nopony. Her words fell flat against the bushy trees, and she started to realize just how alone she was.

Suddenly, the sound of deep, booming laughter echoed through the trees. It sent shivers up Rainbow's spine. Maybe she wasn't so alone after all.... No, it was probably just a trick of her mind. She had to keep moving.

Fifteen minutes later, however, Rainbow Dash hadn't gotten any farther. When she saw the same purple tree with gnarly roots, she realized she had been flying in a giant circle! She needed a better plan if she was ever going to find the entrance to the Spirit Circle before the relic thief.

Rainbow found a safe spot and landed. She hadn't heard the scary laugh again and there had been no signs of anypony else. Something told her that it wouldn't stay that way for long.

"Now where did I put that map of Equestria?" Rainbow said to herself as she riffled through her saddlebag. "I know it's in here somewhere with all this other stuff." Rarity's pair of shoes clanked together and squished into one of the green cupcakes. What had her friends been thinking?

"Yuck!" said Rainbow. She took one of the shoes and flung it behind her carelessly. She expected to hear a thud, but instead she noticed a low gurgling noise, followed by a loud *SNAP*! It sounded like a huge set of teeth.

Rainbow Dash got the funny feeling that she wasn't alone anymore. Her body froze, and she turned around slowly, unsure of what fate had in store for her. What she saw was worse than she'd imagined.

"Ahhh!" Rainbow screamed at a huge pack of Colossa-gators. They had iridescent, scaly green skin and red eyes and were each almost the size of an Ursa Minor. They were like normal alligators, except much stronger and a whole lot different than Pinkie Pie's toothless baby alligator, Gummy, back home. He was so cute.

Rainbow was completely surrounded. She stood frozen in place and watched as they crept toward her. The Colossa-gators were very hungry; they snapped their massive, sharp-toothed jaws and looked her in the eyes. Did they like to eat ponies? She couldn't remember. All signs pointed to yes.

Finally, she got hold of herself. Rainbow flew up into the air, but the thick canopy of low-hanging trees prevented her from getting enough clearance to be safe. She was still within reach of the gators!

"Oh no, you don't!" shouted Rainbow, starting to get angry. She flew around, trying to annoy the giant gators like a tiny pesky housefly. Maybe if she could make them dizzy enough, they'd leave her alone and she could escape! As she weaved through the spiky tree trunks, the gators snapped and chomped. They narrowly missed her rainbow tail more times than she cared to admit.

"Watch this, you ugly gators!" she yelled, flying as fast as she could around them. It looked like a rainbow-colored tornado with random scaly alligator limbs flailing around inside. "That'll teach you to mess with Daring Dash!" Rainbow landed on the back of a huge gator to do a little victory dance. "Ahhh!" she yelled as the big gator swung around, flinging her into the branches of a nearby tree.

She picked herself up and tried to take off again, but her tail was stuck! She yanked and pulled, but nothing worked. The biggest gator of the pack was getting close. He crawled up slowly, like he was savoring his victory. If she didn't break free soon, he would be savoring his lunch—a rainbow Pegasus!

Rainbow looked around for something, *anything* to throw at him. She reached into her saddlebag and grabbed the first thing she could find. It was one of Pinkie's green cupcakes. "If you're so hungry, eat this!" She chucked the baked dessert right into his mouth.

The alligator swallowed the cupcake, burped, and simply walked away. Rainbow couldn't believe her eyes!

What was in those things?! Rainbow reached for another one and gave it a closer look. It had loopy icing that said the words GATOR CUPCAKE on it. Rainbow Dash threw another at a different gator. The same thing happened. They were . . . gator treats?!

"Pinkie Pie, you're a genius!" Rainbow shouted into the air.

Pinkie popped her bushy pink mane out of a nearby tree. "Awww, thanks, Rainbow!"

But luckily, Rainbow was so caught up in the action that she didn't notice her over-eager friend almost blow the cover of the other ponies. Rainbow wasn't supposed to know that they were following her. That would ruin the whole plan!

After Rainbow Dash had gotten rid of all the alligators, she only had one cupcake left. It was the pink one, so she ate it. She hadn't even realized how hungry she was until then. She guessed Pinkie was right about the whole "making room for cupcakes" thing.

It was a minor victory. Even if she was no closer to finding the Half-Gilded Horseshoe, at least a giant creature wasn't eating her for lunch right now. But Rainbow needed to buckle down if she was going to make it to the Spirit Circle by nightfall.

It would help if she had some idea where she was going.

Rainbow finally found her map of Equestria and began to search for any sign of something called a Dual Stronghold like Twilight had mentioned. All she could see beyond the forest were old castle ruins. Rainbow suddenly found herself wishing that Twilight were there. She would have definitely had an idea about where to find the entrance. Or maybe she already had, and Rainbow just hadn't listened…which was entirely possible. Either way, it was too late now.

Rainbow rolled up her map and soldiered on into the unknown.

CHAPTER 11

A Sinking Feeling

★ ★ ★

There was a hint of something glowing and red in the distance. Rainbow watched with curiosity as the glowing mass drifted and swirled through the branches before escaping behind a large shrub. It looked a lot like the green magic smoke Zecora had used to show them the Half-Gilded Horseshoe.

Maybe this meant Rainbow was on the right track!

She took off in the direction of the smoke, hoping that it would lead her closer to the Spirit Circle. "Hey, wait up!" shouted Rainbow as she flew along, relieved that she had a direction to go. Soon she'd find the entrance and retrieve the relic, and Ponyville would be safe once more.

Rainbow reached a large oval-shaped clearing that looked like a lake. But instead of water, the ground below was covered with soft white sand. That was strange. Rainbow hadn't seen sand like that anywhere except at the beach or the swimming hole. She had certainly never seen it in a forest. But the Everfree played by its own mysterious rules, so it made sense in a backward way.

The red smoke hovered over the sand

momentarily before continuing to the other side and disappearing into the woods. Rainbow was about to run after it, when she got a feeling that she shouldn't. She leaped into the air, beating her wings like normal. She soared across the expanse. "Wait up!" she shouted, though she wasn't sure whether blobs of bright red smoke could even hear anything.

She was halfway across when, suddenly, Rainbow felt herself falling! It was as if her wings were frozen in midair. She looked down at the sandy ground. It was approaching fast and there was nothing she could do. Rainbow braced for impact.

"Rainbooooow!" she heard a voice shout. It sounded like...Applejack? It had to be the forest playing tricks on her.

Wooompf! Rainbow Dash landed in the soft sand.

It was a nice cushiony landing. She found herself slowly sinking into its embrace, so she rested a moment. Then, she reached out her right hoof and pulled her body up. Her hoof disappeared into the pale grains of sand. Rainbow tried her left hoof and the same thing happened. Every step she tried to take brought her deeper and deeper into the sinking sand.

"It couldn't be..." Rainbow Dash said aloud, "...quicksand?!"

She tried to spread her wings, but they didn't work. They were still frozen in place by some sort of magic. Now, Rainbow was in up to her knees. If she didn't act fast, the sand would soon swallow her up completely. "This is probably the only time I will ever say this, but—I wish this would go slower!"

Her announcement was met with the

familiar sounds of evil laughter, echoing across the sandy clearing. Rainbow looked around in desperation for something to grab. The edge of the sandpit was about ten trots away. She scanned the foliage and zeroed in on a low, sturdy bush with wiry brambles. If only she had something to reach it... maybe she could pull herself to safety. But what?

"Applejack's rope!" Rainbow yelled out, brightening. "Of course—it's a lasso!"

Luckily, the sand hadn't swallowed Rainbow's saddlebag yet. She reached in, grabbed the lasso, and pitched it up into the air with all her might. She swung it around in a circle like she'd seen her friend do so many times.

Rainbow Dash grunted as she tossed the rope toward the shrub. It bounced off the branches and fell to the dirt. "No!" Rainbow shouted, now waist-deep in sand. It was a lot harder than it looked. She made a mental note to compliment Applejack on her lasso skills when she got home. *If* she got home.

The thought of never seeing her friends again filled Rainbow with a new resolve. There was no way she was going to let that happen! She pulled the lasso in again and gave it another shot. This time, the loop hooked around the bush. Rainbow mustered all her strength and pulled. Inch by inch, she reeled herself back to the solid dirt. By the time she reached the bush, she was exhausted. She collapsed into a heap. This Pegasus had never been happier to have her hooves firmly on the ground.

CHAPTER 12

Finding Your Place

✦ ✦ ✦

After what seemed like an eternity of trotting through the forest, Rainbow finally stopped herself. She wasn't going toward anything, and she had no leads on how to find the Dual Stronghold or the Spirit Circle. She was beginning to wonder if they even existed.

"Dual Stronghold…" Rainbow Dash said out loud, allowing herself to sit on a mossy log. "Dual Stronghold? Hmmm. *Dual* means 'two,' so…two stronghold?"

Rainbow scratched her head. What in Equestria was a two stronghold? Maybe she was getting further from figuring it out than before.

It was starting to get dark.

Time was running out, and Rainbow was starting to feel weary and very alone. She wondered what her friends were doing right now. Applejack was probably having a yummy dinner with Apple Bloom, Big Mac, and Granny Smith. Maybe Fluttershy was reading Angel Bunny an early bedtime story. Twilight might be studying a new spell with Spike. Rarity could have been busy designing a new line of dresses involving utility pockets. And Pinkie Pie was *definitely* baking a giant cake to pop out of—just for fun.

All those things sounded better than being stranded in a scary forest on an aimless mission to retrieve a relic from an unknown thief. Rainbow grabbed Flutter-shy's teddy bear and curled up into a ball. She started to drift off when she heard a voice softly whispering.

"Don't give up, Daring Dash!" it said. "You're supposed to be the bravest pony in Ponyville. You don't want to embarrass yourself, do you?"

"No!" Rainbow popped up and riffled through her saddlebag for her map. She pulled out the Sapphire Stone bookmark that Twilight had given her and stared at it. Why this instead of something useful like

Applejack's lasso or Pinkie Pie's cupcakes? Twilight was usually the most practical one of the bunch. Her gift didn't make any sense.

"I wish this was over!" Rainbow shouted, throwing the bookmark on the ground. She looked down at the gift from Twilight. "I wish I was back with my friends," she whimpered, picking it up and holding it close to her. Why had she pushed them away again? If they were here, this would have been so much easier. She would have already retrieved the horseshoe and Ponyville would be safe. But now she was lost and alone.

"I wish...I were at the Dual Stronghold right now!" And suddenly, a bright white light blinded Rainbow.

Rainbow Dash blinked and rubbed her

eyes with her hoof. When she regained her sight, she saw that she had been magically transported! Instead of being surrounded by spiky, dark trees and low-hanging vines, Rainbow now found herself in front of a large, crumbling stone structure. She knew this place!

"The Castle of the Two Sisters!" Rainbow Dash exclaimed. So that's what *Dual Stronghold* was code for. *Stronghold* was just a fancy word for "castle." If she had figured that out sooner, Rainbow could have saved herself a lot of time and trouble—sneaky Twilight and her enchanted bookmark aside. But there was no time for regrets now.

The Spirit Circle had to be nearby. Rainbow could feel it.

She took off toward the castle, searching for any signs of life. A puff of the swirling

red smoke was just ahead. "Aha! I see you!" Rainbow shouted in triumph, taking off and flying after it. It led her through a maze of winding corridors and staircases that she didn't even know existed. Finally, she ran outside into a grassy clearing. The smoke joined a massive cloud of the same substance. It churned and spun like a slow, red tornado.

"Rainbow Dash!" a voice cried out. "She's here!"

"Don't worry about us!" cried another. "Close the entrance!"

"Fluttershy? Twilight? Is that you?" Rainbow would recognize her friends' voices anywhere. They sounded like they were in trouble, but where were they?

"Finally Daring Dash has arrived!" a

deep voice bellowed. "I wasn't sure if you had survived."

A figure stepped forward but was still shrouded in red smoke. The dark outline heaved with laughter, and a shiver went up Rainbow Dash's spine. It was the same laugh she had been hearing all along.

"Show yourself, you…you…*coward*!" Rainbow squeaked.

"Prepare yourself to be amazed!" the voice cackled. The red smoke parted and out stepped a massive zebra. "For you are graced by the presence of Braze!"

He had blood-red eyes and an earring made of orange-and-yellow phoenix feathers. He had stripes, just like Zecora, only his weren't black-and-white; they were red, orange, and yellow and looked like the flames of a raging fire. It was a bit intimidating.

"I'm not afraid of you, Braze!" Rainbow Dash lied. She narrowed her eyes at him and adjusted her helmet. "Who are you and what have you done with my friends?!"

Braze stepped forward and slowly walked to Rainbow. He looked down at her with a wicked smile. "I knew they would be useful in this endeavor. Open the door, or they're mine forever!" He made a sweeping motion with his hoof to reveal Twilight, Applejack, Fluttershy, Rarity, and Pinkie Pie all tied together with a magical red fire-rope. They were all wearing pith helmets and shirts just like hers.

Rainbow gasped and flew over to them. "What are you ponies doing here?!"

"We're sorry for following you, Rainbow,"

Applejack said. "Honest. We just wanted to make sure you were safe!"

"We tried to let you have your adventure..." Fluttershy added. "But..."

"But then this big meanie zebra caught us and brought us here!" Pinkie Pie pouted, squirming around. Her mane was messier than usual, poking out of her helmet, and she had painted lines across her cheeks like a warrior. "And also, we're all out of cupcakes." Her stomach grumbled loudly. "Which is the worst part!"

"This fire-rope is really frying my mane!" Rarity cried, touching her purple locks. "It's awful!"

"Don't worry, guys! I'll have you free in just a second," Rainbow reached for the fiery rope, but it burned her hoof. "Ouch!"

Braze laughed. "Did you really think

I'd make it that easy? Come here, Daring Dash, this choice will be breezy!" The zebra waved his hoof, and Rainbow found herself being dragged toward him. He turned her around to face a large, freestanding stone door.

It had all sorts of ancient pony carvings across it that seemed to tell a story. There was a Pegasus, who looked a lot like Rainbow Dash, soaring through the clouds with a striped trail behind her. The paint had long since worn off, but it could have been a rainbow. In the middle was a large U-shaped slot. Perfect for a horseshoe. The Half-Gilded Horseshoe. The key that could unleash a ton of scary spirits into Ponyville.

She hated to admit it to herself, but Rainbow was actually nervous.

"Hand over the horseshoe, Braze!" Rainbow demanded, trying to hide her shaky voice. "And release my friends! This is between you...and me!" She stood up a little taller and gritted her teeth. Nopony, or zebra, was going to mess with her friends.

Braze nodded his head, his feather earring swishing back and forth. "Yes, dear Dash, *you* are what I need! It's the only way for your friends to be freed. The spirits will only open the room for the one who can do a Sonic Rainboom."

He tossed the Half-Gilded Horseshoe into the air to show off. It twirled around just as it had in Zecora's green flames. As it glistened and sparkled in the light, Rainbow noticed that the edge caught one of the fire-ropes, cutting it slightly. It was subtle, but it gave Rainbow an idea.

"You want me to open the door to the

Spirit Circle for you?" Rainbow asked, playing along. "And then you'll untie your fire-rope and let my friends go?"

Braze circled around her, little flames escaping from his hooves with each step. "Yes! Yes! Then I'll disappear with my treasure, and you can leave at your leisure." He smirked. Everything was falling into place perfectly.

"Deal!" Rainbow nodded her agreement. A look of horror flashed across Twilight Sparkle's face. Clearly, she thought it was a trick. But Rainbow had a plan.

"Look at that! Aren't you clever? Now insert the key and pull the lever!" Braze salivated, rubbing his hooves together greedily. He tossed Rainbow the Half-Gilded Horseshoe. The ponies all held their breath as Rainbow caught it. Was she really going to open the door? What about the spirits getting out?

If only she could distract Braze somehow....

Rainbow gave a sly wink, and Pinkie Pie seemed to get the hint. "Hey, Mr. Braaaaaaze?" she chirped. "Do you have any snacks?! I'm sooo hungry!"

Braze turned around and growled in rage. "I know nothing of your pony diet! Stop talking for once and just be quiet!"

It had been just enough time for Rainbow to make the switch and slip the Half-Gilded Horseshoe into her saddlebag.

"One haunted room full of treasure, coming right up!" Rainbow said, inserting a regular horseshoe, the gift from Rarity, into the slot. She reached her hooves onto the lever and slowly pulled down.

The Dash to Safety

★ ★ ★

"See? Guess you were wrong!" Rainbow shrugged as she pushed down on the lever again. "It doesn't work." Rainbow Dash's plan was going even better than expected. Braze hadn't noticed the horseshoe had been switched.

"No! No! This cannot be!" Braze looked

toward the sky and let out a deep, angry growl. "I have secured both the Pegasus and the key!"

"Maybe you should just let us go and git along now, Braze," Applejack shouted, struggling against the fire-rope. "Looks like you won't be openin' any spooky doors today."

"Give it up, Braze!" shouted Twilight. "The entrance is going to close any minute and you've got nothing."

"No!" Braze shouted, and began to pace back and forth. He started mumbling to himself, presumably in rhymes. It was the perfect time for Rainbow to make her move. She crept over to her friends, careful not to let Braze see what she was pulling out of her bag. . . .

"The Half-Gilded Horseshoe!" Twilight

exclaimed. "It's been in your bag this whole time?"

"What?!" Braze galloped over and stood between Rainbow and her friends. "I knew that you were being phony! Give it back now, you deceitful little pony!"

Over Braze's shoulder, Rainbow Dash could see that the door was starting to lower into the ground. She just had to buy a little more time and keep the Half-Gilded Horseshoe away from him until it was gone. Then, she would cut her friends free and they could escape!

"I'll never surrender it to you, Braze!" Rainbow shouted. "And in case you forgot— I am the fastest Pegasus around!" Rainbow shot up into the air just as Braze threw a fire-rope at her. It singed the bottom of her tail. Rainbow dived back toward her friends, hoping to cut the rope, but Braze was in the way. He reached out for the horseshoe and almost got it. It was too close.

Rainbow was going to have to do this from afar.

"Hey, Braze! Watch this!" Rainbow hollered. She held the horseshoe up and narrowed her eyes to aim. Then, she flung it like a boomerang—right at her Ponyville friends!

Braze dived for it.

The shoe flew through the air, landing perfectly out of Braze's reach and exactly in position to slice through the fire-rope. It doubled back to Rainbow, as if it were under her control. She caught it with a smirk and blew the residual smoke off its surface. She put it safely away and gave her bag a pat. The girls broke free and cheered.

"All right, Rainbow!" Pinkie Pie squealed, jumping up and down. "Wahoooo!"

"You did it!" said Fluttershy.

"Thank you, darling," said Rarity, smoothing down her purple mane. It still looked perfect.

"Now let's get the hoof outta here," said Rainbow. "This dude is creeping me out." Braze was standing over the door, which had only a few inches left aboveground. He was shaking his head with a pained expression on his face. Finally, the door was sucked into the earth and disappeared. Now, there was just grass. He let out a sob.

"You may have won this time, Daring Dash..." Braze pulled himself up. He looked over to Rainbow, his eyes aflame. "But I will be back to claim my stash! And when the door is back anew...I will not stop till I find you!"

Braze cackled and vanished into a burst of flames.

"And I'll be ready for him," said Rainbow. She wasn't going to let some greedy zebra put her friends or her town in danger again. But maybe next time, she would agree to some help from the get-go. She smiled at her friends. "I mean—*we'll* be ready for him."

"And so, with Braze defeated and the Half-Gilded Horseshoe secured..." said Twilight, quoting a famous line from the Daring Do books, "Ponyville was safe and sound once again, thanks to Daring Dash!"

"...*and* her friends!" said Rainbow Dash proudly. "Thanks for being there, even when I said you shouldn't be. Plus, I couldn't have done it without those gifts! What was with that bookmark?"

"It's a placeholder," Twilight blushed. "I enchanted it to help you find your place."

"And aren't gator treats the best?" Pinkie Pie sighed. "Gummy just loves them."

Rainbow laughed. "You guys really saved my tail."

"It looks a little burned to me," commented Rarity. She inspected where the fire-rope had fried it. "But a trip to Ponyville Day Spa will fix it right up."

"Anything but that!" said Rainbow Dash, shaking her head.

"And you're supposed to be the brave one?" Twilight joked.

CHAPTER 14

The Bravest
Thing

★ ★ ★

Miss Cheerilee's classroom at the Ponyville
Schoolhouse was packed with students from
all over the school. The fillies and colts
were all buzzing with excitement for today's
visitors. The local heroes, Daring Dash and
her loyal friends, were going to talk to the
class about their adventure in the Everfree

Forest. All sorts of crazy rumors had been flying around about exactly what had happened out there, but today they were going to set the record straight.

"My big sister Applejack was there when Daring Dash defeated the evil zebra, Braze!" Apple Bloom bragged to Diamond Tiara, who turned up her nose.

"And so was mine!" said Rarity's little sister, Sweetie Belle.

"Well, I knew Rainbow Dash before she became Daring Dash!" offered Scootaloo, who was wearing her own mini Daring Dash costume.

"All right, let's calm down, my little ponies," Cheerilee said, taking her place at the head of the room. "Let's all give a warm welcome to...Daring Dash!"

"Hey, kids!" Rainbow trotted in and

gave a nervous wave to the students. Every-pony's hooves shot up into the air. They all had questions for the bravest Pegasus in Ponyville. But before Rainbow answered any of them, she had something important to say.

"Remember, it may seem cool to be brave and daring—and it totally is awesome—but if there's one thing I learned as Daring Dash, it's that…"—Rainbow looked to Rarity, Applejack, Twilight, Pinkie Pie, and Fluttershy, and they smiled back—"…sometimes the bravest thing a pony can do is accept help from her friends, even when she doesn't think she needs it!"

Rainbow put on her pith helmet, and the students cheered. "Now who wants to hear a play-by-play of how I was wing-deep in quick-sand and used a lasso to pull myself out?!"